Eugene

**To the oppressed and
downtrodden of the world.**

Never lose hope.

"Beware of the prayers of
the oppressed, for there is
no barrier between them
and God." Bukhari

EUGENE
ABDUL MALIK

Special thanks to:

Ruqayyah Forbes

Rehnaz Mustafa

& Micky Grim

May God bless you always

abdulmalikwriting.co.uk

Email – abdulmalik.writing@gmail.com

Instagram – abdulmalikwriting

Whatsapp – 07931334023

Published by - It's All Love Publications ltd

Cover art by – Sammyart09

Cover design by - Germancreative

ISBN: 978-1-9998432-2-9

Eugene

Abdul Malik

PROLOGUE

A small breeze was enough
To bring
The first thralled leaf
Away from the tall trees
Seasonal seize

It was freezing
Ready for release
Dressed in a garnet shawl
Regardless of the coldness
Letting go was not at all easy

In the dark starlit night
It had been hanging on
For long enough
It knew it had to leave
But until now
Wasn't strong enough

It knew this truth for ages
Still moved through its stages
Refusing to be swayed
Until persuaded
By the brisk whisk of the winds whisper

Which said that there's no doubt
It was made for higher purpose
And it was time for letting go now

Gently
Down
It slowly wound
Until it eventually found
The stony ground

Not the only
Not at all lonely now

It brushed against the rough
Touch of the tarmac
Sliding
Close to where flowers
Softly blossom
Whilst rising
Through the pavement's cuts
Reminding
That from rock bottom
The only way is up

And with that
It was taken up
Whipped into the wind
Way way up
Above the roofs and the trees

High

The city view from height
Is like when the sea reflects the sky
At night

From here
Peace
A masters picture
Lights like splattered glitter
Distant laughs
Chitter
Horns honking on occasion
There's a storm coming
Clouds gathering in congregation

A flock of birds flee
Free
Squabbling through the broken haze

As the leaf
Floats
Like a boat
Bobbing over ocean waves

It floats
Over the woodlands
Where two figures are trekking
A trail leading
Out to an opening
Of grass land
Where a lone bungalow stands

After wonderfully
Riding the wave of the wind
For a few miles
The leaf spirals
And comes to rest on top
Of the bungalow's roof tiles

Beneath
There's a boy sleeping
Tucked into bed
Laying on his side
Right hand under his head

A simple box room
Key in the door lock
Tick-tock of the clock
Prayer mat sprawled on the floor

Neat arrangements
Of old porcelain ornaments
And tournament trophies

Adorning the corner
A sofa with dusty upholstery

A low ceiling
A skylight
Slightly open
Letting the cold breeze in
The sound of slow breathing
Seeping
From the boy sleeping

And then gradually ascending
Over the quiet noises
That the house hides
Noises from two voices
Coming from outside

1. AT THE BUNGALOW

Booom!

His eyes burst open
The thudding at the door
Roars through the walls
Of the whole house
Causing the chandelier to shuffle
He pants in fear
"Discovered"
He pulls off the covers
Jumps up
And slams them on a chair
Near to a plant that's there

Booom!

His feet touch the ground
He looks around
The light from the swinging chandelier
Stretches then shrinks the silhouettes
Which makes a small statue of a deer
Appear like an angry bear

Boom!

The clock on the wall shows the time
To be a five to three
He glances in the mirror
He's thinner than he'd like to be
And blurrier

Boom!

Could never find his glasses when
He needs them most
Small curly fro
Face looks like he's seen a ghost
He'd fell asleep in his clothes
A dirtied white shirt with
The greenest bow tie
He could have chosen
Immaculate cactus green
Cream khakis jeans
Garnished
With a knackered green gaberdine garment
Baggy at the sleeves

His thoughts running a hundredfold
Heart thumping thunderbolts
How could they have come to know
The old country bungalow

He was sure they'd taken proper precaution
To ensure
No opposite forces
Could follow their course in

They'd enforced all
Obvious tactics
In their rush
They even did
Some swapping courses
And doubling backwards

Speeding up
Slowing down
Mirror checks
Surrounding scouts
Opposite signalling
Driving round and round the round about
Without a doubt
No one should have found
Where he was hiding out
No one could have known
Besides...
"Nahh!!??"

Boom!

No time to preen dream or stand and stare

Boom!

The door bubbles
He hears muffled rants and jeers
"Eugene
We know you're in there!"
The phrase that glanced his ears
"It's the muscle"
He whispers to himself
As warm words
Advance from fears
Dance with the cold air
Then disappear

He'd heard much about the muscle

Trouble doubled
Two brothers
That made their hustle
From scuffling thugs
Recovering goods
Covering government crud
And drubbing the love
Out of any lover they could

They were bounty hunters
Hired knuckle
A vile couple
For a minor cup full
You could trust these
Two violent crooks to
Find a needle in a pile of muck
And their style isn't silent or subtle
Eugene scurries to the key hole
And looks through

Boom... boom...boooom!

The door buckles
A foot kicks and cuts through the wood
Like a sword cuts through air
Dust erupts and then...clears
And what appears
A gigantic pair
Standing geared
Grant the beard
And Frank the dank
His sneering angry
Lanky peer

Two titan tyrants towering over 6ft tall
Grant's thick and broad
Built of brick and brawn
Scrunched lips of scorn
As if abhorred
A picture of a boar or pig
His bearded jaw a swarm
Of twigs
A bushy ball of hoar transfixed
With strips of black
The growth of prior
A black that matched both their attire

Feather white flesh
Weathered black leather vests
That look like they're never fresh
The words 'For the city'
Pressed in red letters
On their chests
Left of breast

Frank's a stick
As thin as Grant is thick
His leg sprawled in frozen kick
He's quick
Both tall but Frank more so
Four gangly limbs dangling
From a stalk bony torso
Claws showing
Rings glowing
Pure gold
Also

The wind's blowing
Raw cold
Flinging and throwing
His hair
Which is straw golden
His face expression foretold
More scold

Standing wise
Four ice blue
Scanning eyes
Mischief in all
In seek of fawn
Fists look like their fixed to brawl

They both advance
Stepping over broken planks
And bits of door
That hit the floor
The living room
Is open plan

Frank's first to move in
And search for clues
"Where iz e den"
His words a spew
He slithers past the window
View
The silver moon's light
Spilling through
Which gives the room
A slight tinted hue

"E'z not ere"
Frank exclaimed in blame of Grant
"A waste of time" he claims in rant
Then came a thud from behind the wall
A flickering light
From under the door

"He's in there"
Grant grunts
With head arose
Pointing ahead
At the bedroom
With his long bony turned up nose

A lightning strike
A flashing strip
Which sounds just like
A cracking whip
Rain splatters scatter
Splash and drips
Tapping with a patter pit
On the other side
With panting breath
Squinted eyes and desperate checks
Eugene's trying to find his specs
He finds them laying under the bed

Big black square frames
He places straight upon his face
His vison changes from vague to blade
He scans the room for lest he's bait
Trying to find the best escape

His minds like limbo
Searching for a finite thin glow
In this dark situation
And then 'hope'
He scopes a leaf
A garnet-coloured leaf
Scraping down the sky lights window

A gust of wind
Thrusts it in
Right past his face
It brushes his skin

The door budges
Inward
As the muscle
Try muscling in
They bang
And barge
And push
Until
Splinters bust

"Open up"
They grunt
Teaming
No discussion between them
Just
"Eugene let us in"
Then more buffing and beating
The door nudges forward
Inches
They give it one thrust more

And it
Comes off its hinges
With a roar

The hunters
Come rushing forth
Grant still with
The doors handle
In his pincers

With a single leap
Eugene volts onto the sofa
And hoists onto the shelf
Knocking the trophies over

He pushes open the sky light
Wide enough
For him to squeeze through
Then proceeds to
Climb out
Onto the bungalows steep roof

Grant dives for him
Reaching through
He catches one of Eugene's feet
And pulls
But Eugene does not stop
He kicks himself free
Then moves

He slides down wet tiles
And lands with a thud
On his back
Grant tries to follow
But because of his mass
He gets stuck in the gap

"He's getting away" he flaps
Whilst struggling and shuffling lots
Eugene does not stop
Frank runs back the way he came
To try and cut him off

Eugene
Sprints through the rain towards the woods
At frantic pace
With angry faced Frank
Chasing
Falling behind
Calling his name

"Eugeeene" He calls

Eugene checks the rear
His face showing the fear
"How?" he says to himself
"How could they have known I was here?"

He turns back
Forward
The heart in his core sped
Then…

Buff!

He takes a heavy thud to the forehead

Eugene lay on the floor
As blurred figures
Gather round
Ominous
"How?"
He says to himself again
As he fades out
Of consciousness

2. BEFORE

"Eugene... Eugene!
Eugene come down for dinner before it gets cold"
Not even
The tensed tone pounding of
His mums shouting
From the bottom of the stairs
At the top of her lungs
Could arouse him

He was browsing out of
The window at the slum
The sun clouting
Through an opening in the clouds
The warmth stroking his brow

His focus is down towards the ground
And partly in space
Gazing past his reflection in the glass
Which is cast of just half his face

The park that he's facing
Is a place
Rough sleepers
Have claimed as their base
There are children playing
Hide and seek
In the derelict buildings
On the estate

The estate...
An overcrowded
And dilapidated
Looking place
Encased by
High walls
The barbed wire would thwart an escape

There's a 40ft tall
Chain link gate
Where wardens are placed
And a camera on every corner
Scanning every face

A crew of pigeon's coo
Pecking the pathway
Looking for food
A door opens
A haggard looking dude
Chucks them a few
Slices of bread
Two pigeons
Took them and flew

Eugene grimly watched
The pigeons chase
Nimbly
Around the flimsy chimney pots
Fighting over slices of bread
Which he thought
Could have easily fed the flock

He was lost in thought
His eyes scanned the block
And clocked a boy
With his face covered
Red top
Walking with a bop employed

Rocking towards
A young lady
She's a mum
Pushing a pram
Having fun
With her baby
Engaging in some happy play

Until the boy crossed
A hand span away
Dragged her handbag
Right from her hand
Then ran away
He took off down an ally way

Bystanders stand and gaze
Then carry on talking
The lady watched him vanish
Shook her head in despair
Then carried on walking

Harried
She sends a brave smile into the carriage
Before passing under the window
That Eugene has just managed to open

"Are you okay lady?"
His words aridly spoken
But jarred the poor lady
Into a panic emotion
For a moment...
She looks up
Scopes him
Stood like a stoat
She pulls closed the coat
That had drooped
And was loosely hanging
Around her shoulders

"I am a sinking boat
Who's still afloat"
Wrote all over
Her composure

With a tone raised over traffic sounds
She responds to his question
With a quote
"Karma always comes back around
I was gunna start lashing out
But am with my kid

That bloke might be laughing now
But they say the one laughing last
Is always left laughing loudest"

"Shall I call the authorities?"
Eugene's words of choice

Poised
With a symphony of sympathy
In his voice

"Honestly
Don't worry"
She replies
With a sour face
"No one can afford to pay
A warden's bribe nowadays
Am just getting by"
She says
"Ever since they
Brough me to this place
This is how it stays
And am just tired of
Always... being...
Well...
I'm afraid"

A sigh marches
The phrase
From the darkest
Part of her heart
Like a lone soldier
Scarred but brave
Her eyebrows
Arch...
Then raise

She cries...
Tears bathe
Her wide
Marble shaped eyes
The windows to a heart
Scathed

Eugene
To his surprise
Felt movement
Of his insides
As she cries
Movement like
The prizing open of a door
And the sliding in of skies

Enter
A freight train of blight
He kept a straight face despite
Wanting to offer comfort
But couldn't find
The right insight for plight
To bring brightness
Light

A shake of his head expresses
The blank

They share a silence
Before another short sigh
Suggests that
She had caught sight
Of his short-sighted foresight

Either that or
She felt her core slightly
Embarrassed
By the whole sight

She gathers herself
Uses her sleeve
To banish the grief
That she felt
Creeping down her cheeks

The sounds of the world
Seemed to begin seeping
Back into scene

The sounds of the street
The baby babbling
The crazy gabble
Of the kids
Who are now
Play racing
On the flaky gravel

She looks back at her baby
And smiles bravely
"That dude only stole
His bottle and nappies"
She says
With chords that still sounds shaky
"I better get him home"

She starts to walk her way towards
The corner
Eugene watches
Then calls towards her

"'Lady? What's your name?"
He asks
Crooking his neck round like a hook
To trace her tracks
"Daisy"
She replies without looking back

"And where are you from?"
He shouts
But she was already gone
More questions
Begun to come
And form
On his tongue

He decides
He would run down
He spins round
Watching his feet
Touch down as he catapults off his seat

One step of a run
And **thump...**
He bumps into
His mum

Who's posted like a pillar
In the middle
Of his little bedroom
Her head looming
Over him
Her eyes filled with red fumes
Vex booming
From the stress grooves
On her forehead
Her appointed
Pointing finger
Extended towards the door tread

Her growling glower
Suggests that she was about to pound
Like a pouncing prowler

She shouts…

Eugene feels himself receding
Whilst he's reading her lips
Her mouth forming O's
Whilst pronouncing her vowels

"DOWNSTAIRS NOWWWW!!!"

3. THE LOVERS

It was the smell that he noticed first
Coming down the stairs
His nose is loaded with potent notes of
Flavours as fragrant as
Roses
Another step closer
And smells of fresh dough
Plus
Freshly grown herbs
Meshed with onions and
Garlic
Hearty vegetables
The delectable smell
Of potatoes and parsnips

Pure waves of the aroma
Trawled a trail down the small grey
Patterned wall
Hallway
Which quickened his slowness
The scent of a magnum opus
Had grabbed his focus
And made him remember his hunger
And their home

He shuffled past his mother
His face lit with hope
He drove into the stone floored kitchen
To his little brother
Who is stirring stew at the stove

Unshaken by the approach
Apron over his clothes
Hazel coloured eyes
Smile under his nose
"Ahhh the man of the hour arises"
His brother says in joke
His little face covered in flour
Looking smug as he spoke

"Jerome!?"
Eugene replies
Stark with surprise
Whilst shaking his younger brother
Who is half his size

"Is this real?
I mean how is this real?
How is this possible?
That's proper food
Where did you get all of this stuff?
We're only allowed rations…
Who brought this lot for you?
And what?..."

"Eugene
Stop
Before you blow a fuse"
Their mum says
Looking somewhat amused
At his bemusement

She starts mopping

"Lewis
Brought a box in
This morning
Chocka block with food
And lots of fruits
And said that
Some man
Visiting from the city gave it
In charity...
For the family"

"Yea with real stock cubes"
Jerome includes
As he moves a chair
From under the table
Preparing Eugene
A master's boon
"Please take a seat
I'll be your waiter for this afternoon"

He says
In his most distinguished
Play posh accent that he could blend
Then
He uses his hand as a notepad
And his spoon as a pretend pen

"May I take your order?
You could have more of the porridge or maize
Both all the craze nowadays

Or
I could offer you
Mr four eyes
Always looking goofy
Today's juicy special stew
With dumplings and reeeal stock cubes
Made by yours truly
The choice is yours Eugene"

Eugene looks him in the face
And says swiftly
"Give me my due of the stew
And stop playing games with me"

Jerome
Pouts his lips together
To force his smile to stop
Walks right to the pot
And ladles five sizeable plops
Of the stew into a crock

He serves it to his brother
Wipes a spoon
With a cloth from the sink
Plonks it into the bowl
And asks him
"Tell me... what do you think?'

Eugene stirs it once and then
He puts a heaped spoon of the stew in his mouth
His eyes close
Head shaking
"Umm…Dad would have been proud"

A thought filled silence
Swept through the kitchen
Where everything seemed broken
Clean but broken

Broken bricks in the walls
That are a worn white
Hanging from the ceiling
Broken cords
Broken window
Broken cupboards
A broken back door

The fridge always stayed slightly open
Broken
Broken draws
The only thing
That wasn't broken was the foundation
The floor

"Mummy! Am awake now"
The baby's hazy call breaks the saintly silence
In the place plainly

"Okay baby am coming"
She says
As if she says it daily
She walks over to Jerome
And kisses him on his face
Faintly
"Dad would have been very proud
Of that amazingly tasty plate
That you've made matey"

"And am only 8"
He says
"Yep you're our chef in the making"
"You mean it? I could be a chef"
"Definitely" she says
"With the steps that we're taking
We just need some more ingredients
To keep your methods in training and..."

"Mummy **AM AWAKE!!**"
"Erm
Eugene
When you've finished eating"
She says
"Please don't feel the need to sleep
Go and pop some food to the neighbours
Neither have eaten a proper meal in weeks"

Eugene looks up from his bowl quickly
As she addressed him
He was going to reply first time this time
He'd learnt his lesson
"Yes mum"
"Okay" she says "No forgetting"
She kept his gaze for a few extra seconds
As if inspecting

She was a tall woman
Mary her name
Her skin a rich buttery brown
Which showed little sign of her age
Except a few lines that years of
Smiles and frowns had made

She wore a beautiful but worn
Floral patterned dress
Which flowed flush with the floor
Her aura said
As soft as a petal but also
As sharp as a thorn

And be happy with what God has given you
Natural
Spiritual
She was living proof
Of someone living through difficult times
Whilst keeping the spiritual bit in tune

She would say things like
"If you lose your morals
You lose yourself"
And "love for others what you love for yourself"
Or
"The One is with you
So be with the One"
And
"Keeping calm through your hardships
Will keep you from harm"

The kind of woman people admired
For her style and her grace
And the way she
Carried the weight of the world
With a smile on her face

"MUMMY!!"

The toddler calls
On the verge of a meltdown
Which causes their mum to turn
And disappear up the stairs
As if spellbound

Leaving the boys alone
Jerome sits on the chair
Next to Eugene
And says
In his little voice and tone
"Mum thinks you spend too much time on your own
 And that you daydream too much"

"Yea?
What do you think?"
Eugene asks whilst scooping the last scraping
From the bowls clutch

"Maybe"
Jerome says shrugging his shoulder balls up
"You have been a little vacant lately
I think … I think
You think about home a lot?"
"Sometimes"
Eugene replies
"But recently"
He says
Looking somewhat brazen
"Recently I've been thinking about
Escaping"

"Escaping!!??"
Jerome exclaims

"Yes escaping"
Eugene begins an explanation

"See
You grew up here
So this is all you know there to be
But we used to be free Jerome
We were forced here
From our home
Into plea"

"Arrr
Why can't I remember then"
Jerome groans
As if he'd be rich if he only knew
"You won't remember
When we left bro
You were only two
Remember?"

"Tell me again
Tell me about our home
And how you'd roam
Up to the oak tree view
And the garden that we had
With the flower bed
Where the peonies grew"

"Again?"
Eugene says dropping
His head into a sigh
"Again"
Jerome nods eagerly with his reply

"Okay" he begins
"We lived in the city
Free under the sky
Our house had three floors
Our garden was long and wide

We had an apple tree
A swing
A flower bed of roses and other posies
And of course..."
"Peonies"
Jerome closes

Eugene continues
"After you were born
At the weekend
Mum would stay home with you
And Dad would take us into the woods
An we'd climb up to the oak tree view

We'd pitch a tent looking over the city
And start a fire
Crickets clicking in choir
We'd admire
The sun setting behind the spire

It was nice
Dad would teach us all about life
All his lessons rife
With how to deal with strife

He'd say
Sons
Whenever life gets too much
And you feel that it's fit to tip ya
Come back into nature and reflect
On the bigger picture

By the time you leave
You'll feel a little richer
Than before you came"

He'd say
Plants always grow quicker
During the rain
So
Don't complain

He'd say
Try n embrace every trial you taste
With a smile on your face
Because
After every storm
The sunshine feels greatest

Or was it
We appreciate
The suns warmth
More after the storm

I can't remember which way he'd say it
But the basic point
Of every point
That he made was
Being patient

I try to be patient
With all that I have in me
Dad was so positive
Honestly Jerome
You're way more like Dad than me"

Jerome grins
Listening
With the interest of a fan
Both his elbows on the table
His chin resting in both hands

Eugene continues
"Mum and Dad would team up
And cook the most supreme grub
You've ever seen bruv
And tasty
They would
Invite all the neighbours to eat
And it was…
It was real love
No handouts then
Now it's all slanted
We took it all for granted then

I remember when we embraced
The religion of love
And became lovers
Joining
Sisters and bothers
Of all financial degrees
And colours
Instructions?
To bring ease and peace to others

Until that small violent group
Came with the vibe of war
Killing
Then
Claiming to be lovers
But I don't think
They felt love inside at all

They were the militant type
We knew they weren't real lovers
Because
Lovers are forbidden
From taking innocent life

We condemned them
We fought them
We despised them
But despite it all
The screen teams
Still swiped us
With the same brush
To describe all lovers as
Undesirables

When Dean Jiles became world leader
He decided to confine us all
Hordes of lovers
Who wouldn't hurt a fly
Confined
Behind giant walls

Ghettos
Or estates
Especially made for us
And a few days after he gave the order
They came for us

They did this to lovers all around the globe

You were too young to remember"
He says

"I remember though
Those wardens
Their forbidding footsteps
Crunching
Through the December snow
Their tempered eyes
Venturing with an ember glow
Steam venting from
Densely clothed sentry's
They didn't force entry
No
For 'The City' emblem
Presented
Then
They entered our homes

Those who contested
And protested
Were still arrested
But with extras
So
Mum wisely requested
We stay calm as they oppressed us

She said that
We will always be free
As long
As we remain collected
And keep our hearts
Connected to the One

Five years
We've been living here
Two years since Dad's disappeared
All of us live in fear
Getting nowhere
Just sitting here

I am sick of being passive
So
Jerome
My dear brother
And clever little mate
I
Am
Going to
Escape"

"What about us?" Jerome says
"What about you?" Eugene replies
"You know I work alone bro
Am a lone ranger
And no stranger
To close danger
I don't need anybody"

He claims
Pushing the empty bowl forward
Before throwing the spoon into it
"We're born alone
And we die alone
So
We'd best get used to it"

"How do you propose to escape?"
Jerome asks in his vibrant excited tone
"I don't know little brother"
Eugene replies
"I don't know"

Clank!! Clank!! Clank!!

A burst of urgent tapping
The sound of metal clapping at the window
They both jump
"Who is it?!"
Eugene shouts
Before its cracking crescendo

"Open the door"
A rugged voice replies
From outside
The boys watch wide eyed
As the handle is tried
Frantically
"Eugene
Open the door"
The voice shouts more angrily

Jerome looks anxious
"Lewis?"
Eugene asks
His language laced with anguish

"It's me" Lewis answers
"Open the door! Quick"
Eugene brings
The motion of the key
To the still of the door
Click!

Lewis storms in and
Slams the door closed
With such force
That Eugene's
Thin frame is almost thrown to the floor

"What's going on?" Eugene says
Slightly hurt and stroking his leg
As Lewis pulls his
Hoody off over his head
Exposing his vest

Which he pulls proper over his chest
He moves his face close to the door
Until the wood is pressed to his flesh

"Shhh" he says
As if listening closely
One long finger on his lips
A slight redness in both cheeks

Light tired pitted eyes
Which fit with his gritty vibe
Dark wired stubble
On both sides of his wide jaw
Untidy

"Lewis? what's happening"
Eugene's enquiry
A quieter concern now
Lewis responds loudly
With a silent but stern frown

"Shhh" says Jerome
Whose ears are pricked like he heard something
The thudding like sound of running
He whispers
"Somebody's coming"

The sound of jogging footsteps
Loom closer
Heavy legged
Boots booming
Approaching like troops or soldiers

The sound
Echoing
Through the enclosure
Like doom

They stop near the door
Breathing breath at a quick pace
One says to the rest
"I could've sworn I seen him go this way"

The footsteps
As quick as they came
They fade

Eugene looks down
At where Lewis has placed his swag
Dumped under the jumper
Is what looks like Daisy's bag

4. MORTIMER

"Dad is Dead!"
Lewis's claim
Quietly exclaimed
His words fired in a way
To try an maintain privacy
Their mum's room is beside
And he's entirely
Frightful of notoriety

They had left Jerome
Tidying
Despite his pleas
To follow his big brothers
Upstairs
The only invite for him
Was stay downstairs
Or there would be no more stew
Or anything of the like for him

Their bedroom was dim
Light
Poking through either side
Of
Slowly swaying curtains
Which Lewis had closed
On arriving in

The window still open
From when Eugene
Was sighting him
Pirating

Items from
Daisy's power pink
Flower print
Bag are scattered
Flung across
The bottom bunk

A half full
Baby bottle
Nappies and
Some other junk

"Dad may be dead
Lewis"
Eugene says
"But we still have to
Respect what he conveyed
Plus
He's only dead
When we forget
The lessons that he gave"

Lewis steps
Close to his face
His hot breath
Steaming the two screens
Of Eugene's specs

"Spare me the stories of Dads piety"
He says
"How can anyone survive acting righteously
In this society?
Dad taught me to provide
So I'll provide anyway I can"

"By stealing?" Eugene interjects
Pushing away his stance

"Dads heart was love
Being 'Robin Hood' was not his way
He worked hard for us"

"Everyone has their own way" Lewis says
"But some ways" Eugene debates
"Bring more harm than good"

"It's harm enough
Watching your loved one's starving
Whilst wardens are bringing carts n trucks
Of food into the estate for themselves
With no regard for us

We've been discarded
Like garbage
Eugene
I hate to think
What they've got on the cards for us

The last time
I saw this sort of enforcement
Supported by media distortions
Of a people
Was in school when we
Learned about
The war
That tore up
Europe
In the 1940's"
Lewis says

He closes his flow
Just as he hears
Commotion coming
From the road below

The sound of a car parking
Orders being barked

Lewis's face calms
He steps back
One hand tucks into his pocket
He walks towards the window
And stood
His other palm clutches
The curtain
And pulls it
Just
Enough
For him to peek a look
At the street

Wardens
He sees them
Pacing the pavement
Weaving through a sea of
Feeble
Meek looking people
Like a shiver of sharks
Seeking food

He sees
The deep blue
Uniforms of
The weapon wielding wardens
That gave him chase

The wardens
A group of meaty sized
Seedy guys
With beady eyes
Seeking him
Like beagles
Pushing and shoving people
To make way

At least
Four of the wardens
That usually patrol
The borders
To keep order
Had aborted their posts
And were also absorbed
In sorting
And
Searching
To
 "Seize that thief"

"Seize that thief!"

Was the audible call
Of the chief warden
Clean shaven
Mean faced
Mortimer his name

His call
Was from the
The rear window
Of the jeep
That had pulled up
A few seconds before

The door opens
One black loafer
Touches the floor
His tall broad frame
Folds out

A coldness sprouts
His boldness
Seemed to hold
All bodies to order
All eyes on him
Closed mouths
Fear filled awe

He wore a
Long black
Double breasted
Corduroy overcoat
Which matched
A black
Fedora hat

That
Slightly
Obscured
The view of
His venom cold eyes
White shirt
Red
Seven-fold tie
Pure carnivore aura

He was roaring orders
His talk is quick
Poking holes in the air
Directing the wardens
With his walking stick
Whilst walking
Towards the corner

**"DADDY
I TOLD** you

To wait for **ME!"**

Says the voice of a smaller caller
Clambering out the rear seat
Of the jeep
His daughter

About 8 years old
Clothed like a princess
Silver and pink dress
Light glaring
Off the
Sterling gold
Earrings
She's wearing

Her brown
Hair in
Platted pigtails
Chubby cheeks
Face as though
She is gearing
For domineering

Bossy
Poking the air
In the direction
Of her parent
Until she is
Stood near him
She's the only one
Who appears
Unfazed by his appearance

"You said you were
Taking me to the city fair
So whhhy are we here?"
She shouts at her father
Further
As if she was the master
And he was the learner

Mortimer kneels
Strokes her face
And says
"Missy
We'll go as soon
As we handle
This business for the city"

"What have you done?"
Eugene asks
Looking uncertain
Whilst
Standing near his older brother
Peering through the other curtain

"This doesn't seem right at all
All this because you snatched
The bag of an undesirable?"

Lewis lets out a sigh
And shakes his head
"You're right" he says
"There's more

This morning
I went walking
Whilst it was still dark
And stumbled
Upon the carpark
Where the wardens
Have their food storage cart parked

It was unattended
And I was tempted
By hunger
And hard luck
I took their last box
And scarpered
But I forgot to pull my scarf up

I must have got caught by their cameras
And obviously hadn't considered
Changing my clothes
I didn't think of the damage
That could have arose
Just of the pros
And I know how it'll go from now"

Eugene looks back down
At Mortimer through
The tiny gap in the curtain
As Mortimer's eyes
Rose up
And seemed to lock with his
Eugene caught the vibe
And froze up

Mortimer mimed the words
That all three of them thought
"Thieves always get caught"

5. THE VISIT

Lewis backs against the wall
Looking timid
Small and pitiful
"I have to get out of here"
He mutters
"Otherwise
They'll kill us all"

Eugene's lips quiver
His body delivers
A sure shiver
Spawned by
The thought
That Mortimer
May have
Caught a glimmer

Lewis recovers his pose
He hurriedly claws
Through a cupboard
And rummages draws
Bundling clothes
Into a backpack that
He had chucked on the floor

"If I leave now
There's a chance
I won't get caught
There are no wardens at the watch towers
And no patrols at the check point

I'll go out the back
And sneak past them
To avoid confronting Morty
I could cover a lot of ground
Before those grunts
Come hunting for me"

"That's crazy
Where will you go?"
Eugene says
In the same
Panic tone as his
Brothers voice
"I don't know"
Lewis replies
"But we haven't got
No other choice"

Eugene peeks out the window
And sees the wardens
Marching towards them

Harsh
Whilst
Mortimer
And
His daughter
Follow
Talking
Like it's a calm
Walk in the park

The sea of people
Parting
Wider
Every time they
Step a foot
People at their windows
Everybody
Trying to get a look

"They're coming Lewis"
Eugene barks
Whilst turning his head quick
Lewis is dressed
Bag on his back
Head dipped
Stepping out of the exit

He legged it
Round
And
Down
The winding
Stair case
Gliding

Eugene
Strides behind him
At a fair pace
Colliding
With the sides
Sending
A clear vase of
White
Roses
Flying

Their mum
Rushes out
The room
She had resided in
Enquiring the sounds
A smiling baby
Bound to her side
Excited by the ride out

"What's happening?
What's going on?"
Their mother cries out
Trying to find out
As she strides down
Following her boys
Into the kitchen
Receiving no reply

She was racing in pursuit
Lewis takes the
Remaining of the stew
Off the table
That Jerome had placed
Into two
Small container
For the neighbors

He lifts a
Brown box
Which had
An assortment
Of different food in it
And places the
Two containers of stew into it

Jerome
Is in the kitchen
Sitting
Positioned at the table
Sipping
Something sweet
From a beaker
With a picture of
Great Britain
On the label

"Tell the neighbours
I said
Why thank you very much"
He says
Standing
As he moves the stool
Still smug about his stew
Face looking
As cool as a fool
In school

He wipes some drool
From his chin
That was dribbling off his face
Realizing
That everyone had stopped to watch him
His face drops
"What?" he says

Their mum
Loses her patience
And
Props the baby
On the table top
From off her waist
She dives across
The space
Towards the exit
That Lewis is facing
And blocks his way

Lewis
In his haste
Tries to
Slip through
Her pose
But she
Skillfully
Grips
A fist full
Of his clothes

"Those wardens out there"
She says
"Are they coming for you?
What did you do?
Was it the food?
I knew it was too good to be true

Please look at me when
Am speaking to you
Son?
Please"

She pleads

Her face
A still portrait
An array of calm rays
But
Underneath
Her hearts blazing
Heart break

Lewis's
Head raises
His eyes
Meet her gaze
His size
Just a foot higher
Then her frame

"I've let you down mum"
He says
"I am sorry"
He takes her hand
And kisses her skin
Softly

She's
Speechless
For a second
Then she reaches up
To caress his cheek

"My baby"
She says
Shaking her head in disbelief

As the distant beat
Of footsteps
That hit the street
Cease
And change
Into deep grisly breathed
Whispers
Outside

Her lips repeat
"My baby"

As fists
Beat
The door
Like a drum
And a warden calls
"Open up for the city"

She bends
In reach of a low draw
Which she opens
With a quick release

"My baby"
Again
Her lips repeat

She flicks out an old
Hole filled
Oak Brown
Cloak
Like a blanket
And lifts
It round and
Over him
It molds to his shoulders
"So you don't get cold"
She says
Her words console
The woe that is on show in him

He nods
Then turns the nob
On the back door
Which opens
With a croaky swing

He turns to Eugene
Who is now focusing
Down the hall
At the front door
That the wardens
Are close
To opening

"Let's go Eugene"
Lewis says
Signaling
To his bro to go with him

"Go?
He's not going with you"

Their mum says
Stood with
Panic
Stricken emotions
Potent in her
A slight croak
In her throat
Her words spoken
In a broken rhythm
Loaded with
A sense of foreboding

"Lewis!
Just go!
Now!"
Her words
Break out
With a heavy heave

"No matter
Where you go
Just know
A mother's love
Never leaves"

As the back door
Closes
Lewis's
Fleeing foot steps
Echo
As they tread the street
Whilst
The front door
Opens with a
Very slow
And steady creak

6. EXECUTION

"Oopsi"
Mortimer says
As he peeks a look
To see
Into the house
At the setting

"It seems somebody
Left the door unlocked
Do you
Mind if we…
Step in?"

The politely posed question causes
The family
To pause with their jaws dropped
All shocked
At his presence
And the pleasance in his suggestion

"Thought not"
He says
Menacingly
"I mean
Of course not"
His mimicked
Heavenly politeness restored

"You undesirables
Would never leave
Somebody hanging at the door
Would ya

No
You wouldn't"
He says
Whilst he's entering

"Not with all ya morals and ya ethics
And all of ya other disgusting sentiments"

The wardens
Stay at the door
Standing steady at the ready
A deadly looking
Medley of hot sweaty
Pot belly
Heavies

"Gentlemen"
Mortimer turned and said to them
Gesturing
In their direction
A request for them to enter in

Their entering sends
Tremendous
Tremors trembling
Through the small house
Mary
Pulls the kids closer
As wardens
Begin to scout

Dispersing
Upstairs
Downstairs
Steadily
Searching
Every niche they're able
Whilst
Mortimer and his daughter
Take up perch
At the kitchen table

As he rests his hat on
It's hard-wooden surface
His dark curly hair
Swirls
Into a
Face full of serpent purposes

"Why so nervous my child"
He says to Eugene
With slithering style
His guile
Behind a
Vile
Sinister smile

"What's your name?"
He asks
Eugene gives him a straight answer
"And your age?"
"13"
Eugene responds
In the same plain manner

Mary steps forwards
Drawing Eugene
Round behind her back
Her head scarf wafting
Through the draught
That is riding past

"What do you want Mortimer?"
She asks
With soft smile and stern tone
Fixing her scarf
That the wind from
The open door had blown

"Yea what do you want"
Jerome says
His head peering
Out from behind
His mother's legs
Sticking his tongue out at Missy
Who responds with the mirror effect

"Well"
Mortimer says
Sitting back in his chair
"I was on my way
To take our Missy here
To the city fair

When I received
Some rather
Unfortunate news
Of a thief
Leaving my men without food
And disappearing
Somewhere
In this area

And normally
When a search is composed
I catch the things
That my troops might miss
And
When I came
I thought
I would like to meet
The family
With
Curtain closed
On an amazing
Afternoon like this

So…
Here we are
Coursing"
He looks around the room

"Nice interior
It's clear to me
You undesirables
Really are inferior
Look at this place"
He pokes
His finger into a tear
At the rear of the
Chair's cloth exterior

"Not even fit for a dog"

He snarls
As he glares a serious
Look of contempt
Towards Mary
Who is standing there
Staring back at him
With an airy calm
A banging upstairs
Scares the baby
Who plants her face
Into Mary's arms

"Despite what you've told
The world"
She says
"We didn't come here by our own choosing
You've forced us here
This whole situation
Is your abusing

We're dying under these conditions
And only just surviving
On the food you give us
You've imprisoned us
Without any crime"

"But you undesirables
Are always smiling"
Mortimer says
His coal eyes prying
With a cold connive

"We smile
Because we have hope"
She replies
"Our faith keeps our souls alive

"Faith?"
He laughs
"Faith is the problem we have with you guys
Put your faith and hopes
In us and we'll
Arrange a feast for you and your family tonight
We'll give you amnesty rights
A way out of this travesty?"

"I'd rather die" she says
"Than trade faith
For a taste of your vanity
Paradise lays in wait for those
Patient in the face of calamity
We're for humanity
You're all for yourselves
We could never betray the love
For your selfish insanity"

"This thief
He's your son isn't he?"
Mortimer says suspiciously
As one of the wardens
From the infantry
Returns to report
On the missing thief

"He's not here sir"
The warden says
Gingerly
"Call the hunters
Instantly"
Mortimer growls
Viciously

"He's probably
Over the wall
The little sneak
Call the muscle in
Tell them to be tough with him
And rough him up enough
To deter other ruffians

But
I want him alive
So I can make an example of him
And give any other aspiring runners
A sample of how we trample on them

Sound the Alarm" he says
And alarms begin blaring
Tearing through the air
Mary steps toward Mortimer
In a flare of daring

"They're only kids"
She declares
"And hungry ones at that
How could you
Be so cold
To want to put
Bounty hunters
On his track"

"Well
Obviously"
Mortimer responds
"It's a question of respecting authority
And policies and making sure we're
Following legal procedures properly

And honestly
The pay is to die for
And when
His highness
Dean Jiles
Finds out how much I've sacrificed
For him

And how many
Lover's schemes
I've foiled
My name and fame
Will rise
More
Maybe he'll make
Me secretary or better yet
Right hand for him"

"Daddy
Let's go now!"
Demands Missy
Looking around
Prissily
Tugging her father's hand
He stands from his seat
"Wait baby
Daddy's busy

Your son will be
Caught and
He will be killed
For his crimes
But don't worry
All of you
Undesirables will follow
Suit in due time

Our screen teams are doing great work
To ensure that you are all firmly hated
We're just waiting for the order
And you vermin will be exterminated"

"Exterminated!?
What do you mean exterminated?"
Mary exclaims

"Soon you'll see how
Having hopes in other than us
Are merely in vain"
Mortimer says

He takes his hat from the table
Where he had left it
Puts his stick under his armpit
And steps forward towards the back exit

"I assume he made good his
Great escape through this door?"
He says
As he strides past Mary
Whist straightening
The coat that he wore

"Gentlemen"
He calls to
The wardens
Who proceed to move
At a super speed
The burly bodied
Wardens pour
Into the small kitchen
Until there's hardly any room to breathe

Then
They leave
One by one
Through the back door
Which Mortimer
Slams closed
To complete the intrusion
"I'll be back
Quicker than you can say
Execution"
He laughs

7.ESCAPE

Finally
They left them alone
Leaving them
With just scent and silence
They left their home
With the aroma of
Sweat and expensive cologne
And a sense of extra brokenness

"He said that we will be silenced"
Mary says in a tone
That suggests she's reflecting

She's in a mode opposite
To Jerome's
Who's flexing himself in response
"Did you see me
Eugene?
I was like
Yea
Mortimer
What do you want?"

He laughs
Whilst reenacting the scene
With overacting

Eugene's
Sat
Gasping
Both hands
In his lap
His reaction
As if he was
Trying to grasp
The recent happening

"I don't think
You heard what he said Jerome"
Eugene states
"Bruv
They're planning to
Erase us
They want to wipe us out
Terminate
Eradicate us"

"Wait
Do you mean?"
Jerome says
Stopping in his steps
"Yes"
Eugene says
Drawing his fingers
Across his neck

"Do you think that he's serious
Or just saying it to scare us?"
Jerome says

"I think a bit of both"
Eugene returns
"But
To be fair it's
Something Lewis
Has been trying to declare
To us for years
And now we've heard
It with our own ears
I think it's clear that

We have to escape this nasty estate
And at the quickest pace
To warn the masses
Of what the elite classes
Plan to initiate

This might be
Our only chance
We have to be
Quick" he says
"Whilst they're chasing Lewis
We could literally
Just skip the gate"

"Crazy talk"
Jerome says
"No ones
Ever escaped before"

"Its fate"
Eugene says

His face in awe
His hand
Pointing
Down the hall
Towards
The brilliant blinding light
Shining through the open door

Where the breeze
Had brought leaves in
That strolled onto the floor
Of the passage way
Like roaming rovers
People
Peeping in as they pass
Checking to see if
The action is over

The gaps
Between
The passing folks shoulders
Expose
A straight road
Leading to
The distant
Check point

Where there is no patrol
At the fenced gate
Which joins with the walls
And goes straight up

40ft
Tall

Closed
And imposing

Rose red sirens
Whirling
Either side of it
In sight between the flats
The sound
Exploding
Through
The whole enclosure
Whining like crying cats

Mary sat at the table
Staring into space
The considering on her face
Shows
She's figuring an equation

"Eugene's right"
She says
"We have to get a message out
But how?
It's not like they'll
Just let us out

An attempt to escape
With the baby
Would be a bad mistake
We'd be captured straight away
We'd never make it past the gate

And with Jerome?"
Jerome looks at her with hope
"No"
She groans

"Well then"
Eugene says
"I'll just have to go alone"

"Out of the question"
She spouts at his suggestion
"You'll be captured and arrested
And subject to their aggression"

Eugene looks her in the face
"Mum
I can make it
You always say
When the One
Gives us the stage
To do good
We should take it

We have information
On how they're
Planning the most despicable of evil
And if what he says is true
We must warn the people

A decision for us to all
Stay here with you
Could be lethal"
Mary sits back in her seat
"Am just thinking about your father"
She says
"What would he say?
What would he do?"

"I think he would agree with me too"
Says Eugene
"He'd see a pattern
To this sequence
He'd say that
Everything that happens
Always happens for a reason

Dad said
When facing
The worst evil
We should
Serve people
An I think
The best way to serve
And avert hurt
In this event
Is to alert people

City folk
Think we're here for
Work and education
They have no idea
Of this debasing
That we're facing"

Mary
Breathes a sigh
Of defeat

"Okay" she says
"Say you make it to the gate
Without being
Stopped
And then you manage
To scale over
The fence top

And then somehow
You navigate
Across the forest scape
Bravely
And make it
To the city gate safely…
Then what?"

"Well then…" he says
"Well
Am sure there's still a lot of peaceful people
Out there that I could seek to speak to"

"But to find someone
That will believe you?"
She says
"Will be no easy thing to do"

"We have to try"
He says
"We have to strive
Or we might be smothered
Besides
You taught us
That love is about
Sacrificing
To give life to others

We have to uncover
This oppression of the lovers
But I won't try to run
Without the blessing of my mother"

Mary sighs
After seeing what Eugene's eye contained
She smiles at him lovingly
The type that would disguise her pain
"My God
How the time flies"
She says
"And how you boys have grown
And changed
One thing we must know is that
Nothing ever stays the same

Good days come and fade
Hard days do the same
So
We live with love
In faith that
Good times will come again"

She says as she
Walks over to the fridge
Which she opens
With a slow drastic drag
She takes hold of three
Stone cold
Brown
Bread rolls
And places them
Into a plastic bag

She grabs
A small metal flask
They had
On a shelf
At the rooms border
And fills it with the water
From a barrel that is in the corner

She plugs it with a cork
To stop the water spilling
On the ride
But couldn't cork the mourn
That is slowly
Spilling from her eyes

She wipes them
Dry
Before turning back
Then she gives
Eugene the bag of bread
A smile
And the flask

"Just make sure you return back to us
In one piece"
"Yes mum
I will"
He responds
Whilst dragging his shoes
Onto his feet

He looks up
And sees the struggled
Look in her face
He hugs her
And feels the safety in her
Loving embrace

"Remember God
Always"
Mary says
Whispering
The things she thought
"Any good you intend
The One is with you
In support"

"I love you all"
Eugene says
With full love and loyalty
He takes Mary's hand
And kisses her skin
 Like she's royalty

"We love you too"
Mary says
Whilst handing him
An old green gabardine fleece
"So you don't get cold"
She adds
Eugene takes it
Slowly

"Don't forget your prayers"
She says
"Keep yourself connected
Show respect to the One
And you will always be protected"

"I want to say something"
Jerome says
With his
Arms in reach
Seeking
Eugene's ear
Eugene bends
To hear him speak

His bony cheek
Against Jerome's

Jerome
Says one word
That lights Eugene's face wholly
With a smile
That shows his teeth

"Peonies"
Jerome says
"Yea
Peonies"
Eugene repeats

"I have to go"
He says
As he stands
Straight
And boldly
He threads
His hands
Through
The arm holes
Of the fleece
He's holding

Stood at the door
Eyes fixed on the skies
As if his mind
Is beholding events unfolding
The jolting
Sound of sirens
Pulsing
Un-halting

He steps out onto the road
His family
Watching him
As he goes
Walking
Then marching
Like a solider
Wind rustling through his clothes

The people stand
Frozen
Wonder
Is what their
Feature's display
As Eugene strides towards
The gate
Which is about 200 meters away

A lone warden
Watching
Suspects
The intent
In Eugene's face

He yells
"Hey
Where you going
Oi
You…Heey"

And then
Eugene bolts
Like a bullet from a colt
Running
Breath
Pulling in
Then blowing out
Thundering

His body felt
The punishing assault
His fast feet
Covering the asphalt
He dashes between the
Park and the old derelict flats
Flying past like a flash
He blasts down the back road

No sign of slowing his rate
Focused on the gate
Cameras
Rotate
To keep him
In focus
But he keeps on going
Straight

"Stop!"
The warden calls
He's now
Chasing him
But gives up
After a few meters
Of struggling
To keep pace with him

Eugene
Racing
Facing the ascent that's due
His head raising
Higher and higher
As he tries to keep the
Top of the fence in view

He comes close and jumps
Leaping like a brave sphynx
And clings to the fence
His fingers slot through the chain links

He clambers towards the top
The world getting smaller
The further he goes
Looking downward at the drop
His mind swirls slow with vertigo

His feet slip
His hanging
Dangling legs fatigued
They crash into the fence
Which rattles like a set of keys

Rattling like
The sound of freedom
More reason
To try and find his feet
Just a little bit further
And his journey to the top
Complete

He scarpers higher
Until he reaches
The razor sharp
Barbed wire
That he'd
Sited
From his bedroom prior

He reaches and pulls it
It digs and scraps him
It takes away skin
A little blood escapes him
But he's not concerned about
The cuts it gave him
Just with liberation
He tugs the wire cumber
He tugs until it comes loose
He tugs it just enough
To make a space
For him to duck under

And lumber himself
Over onto
The other side
To the front
Where he looks
And sees the whole
Estate staring
At his stunt
Cheering

With Mortimer and his grunts
Looking ruffled
In the distance
Their muffled shouts
Insistent
"Eugene come back this instant"

Eugene doesn't listen
He tightens his grip
On the fence
And the viciousness in their voices
Makes him quicken his descent
Scrambling down
The fence rattling
As he travels
And as he comes close
To the ground
He jumps
Crunching onto the gravel

He swivels round
To a winding road
With woodland either side of it
"Which way now?"
He says to himself
Trying to decide
Which route
Has the best survival promise

No time for standing idle
He strides towards
The undergrowth
And dives
Through a bush
Of ivy
And stinging nettles
Which sting
Through his clothes

As he heads deeper
Into the woods
Weaving between the trees
And coarse bushes
To make best his head start
He hears Mortimer's voice
On the estate Loud speaker
"You won't get far Eugene
You won't get far!"

8. ALONE

Like a lone shadow
Eugene trundles through the woods
Ducking under branches
Fallen leaves
Crumpling under foot

He pushes bushes
To make a way
In the darkness
That had consumed
The night had over taken day
The only light
Is from the moon

Its light
Slipped through slits
Between the leaves
Of the canopy
And dressed parts of the
Woodland in a tapestry of majesty

The air filled with a natural mist
The temperature is dropping
The sound of chirps
Groans and clicks
The sense that all is watching

As hours pass
Weariness
Begins hassling his might
But he knew
The best chance
He has
Is travelling by night

So despite fatigue
He struggles on
Until he could no more
Then finds a spot
Between some shrubs
And lumbers to the floor

He thinks about
His family and how he'd
Never actually been alone
And what they would be doing
If they were all back at their home

He thinks about the future
And how he is to face it
And how every single person
Has the power to reshape it

He rummages
In his plastic bag
And scoffs the rolls of bread
He takes a sip of water
Then nurses the hand that bled

He watches the reddish sky
Of dawn deposing
Darkness and its wonder
Then with heavy eyelids
Drawing closed
He falls into a slumber

9. TRUST

"Do not move a muscle"

It's morning

Eugene wakes
To a gruff voice

He's facing
Two large
Black
Rough
Muddy
Moist
Scuffed boots
Standing
About a centimeter close

His out of focus vision
Moves up
To see that the boots belong
To a rather large dude
Stood
With blue cut jeans
And a checkered green shirt
Loosely tucked

A goatee beard
35 or maybe older
Black braided hair
That cascade
On to broad bolder shoulders

His face focused
On Eugene

Dark eyes
His stance
Frozen cold

Ready to clout
His chest puffed out
A tough
Stout
Looking chap
With a rusty axe
An axe that he had
Hovering above his
Hood and
Black woolly
Skull cap

Sleeves rolled up
On beefy arms
That are
Cocked back fully

Preparing to drop
The axe and chop

Eugene shuffles forward
To avoid
Being quartered
And cleaved
"I said don't move"
The man repeats
More forcefully

As he raises
The axe
To the blues skies
To rain down
A strike
And hew
A snake rises
From the grass
Dives to take a bite of Eugene
But the guy strikes
And slices
The snake right in two

"Arghhhh"
Eugene screams
The man grunts a laugh
"Sorry to frighten you"
He says
His persona brightens
As he offers Eugene a hand
And the
'I'll help you to climb up' cue

Eugene declines
And begins to stand on his own

"Was that a viper?"
He asks
Whilst rising to
"Nope just an adder"
The guy replies
"Not lethal
But still
Not nice if it takes a bite of you"

"I thought you were a bounty hunter"
Eugene says
Whilst softly
Dusting his clothes off
The sun had fully risen
Bird songs aloft

"A hunter? Me? Ha"
The man grunts
"Am I really that ugly?
I am a lover
Born and free"
He says proudly
His tough face
Warms with some sort of glee

"You're … free?"
Eugene asks

"Well"
The man pauses
"Let's say
We're as free as we can be
But not as free as we ought to be
Am sure if
One of those hunters
Or wardens see
That we're walking free
They would want to
Cut our freedom short
And sweet
They'd throw us
Into one of those ghettoes
Quicker than you could say
Don't throw away the key"

"We?"
Eugene asks
"There are more who are free?"

"We?
Did I say we?"
The man says morbidly
"Always too much
Talking
Me

Anyway
What's your story?"
He says switching attention
Back to Eugene
"Why are you out here
Why were you
On the floor …
Asleep?"

His ball bean eyes
Look at Eugene
A little more cautiously
His enormous palms
Rubbing the black coarse hair
On his cheeks

"I
Erm" Eugene stutters
As he thinks audibly

"I…"
He begins talking
Before
His speech is obscured
By the sound of
Branches cracking
Under footsteps
Coming towards them
On a near path
"Wait"
The man says
Grabbing
Eugene back
"Did you hear that?"

They both freeze

They hear the voice of men
Discussing
Something
About
Running
And cunning folk

The man pokes
His face through
A bush to see
Who is coming
Close

He
Retracts

"Whoa
Wardens
Three of them" He says
Whilst moving back
And crouching behind a tree
Slowly
"I've never even seen one
In these parts
Never mind a trio"

"They're looking for me"
Eugene spoke
His fear shared with surety
He stands with his back
Against a tall sycamore tree

He peeks
Around its trunk
To watch
The wardens wander past
But sees that
His plastic
Bag had blown
Onto the path

It was too late to grab it
"Don't panic"
The man whispers from his vantage
With a finger on smiling lips
His axe
He had on brandish

As Eugene
Turns away
Thinking about
A fate of
Being poached
He listens to the wardens
Converse
As they approach

"I didn't mean to annoy
Or for my talk
To cause offense"
One of them says
"I just
Still cant believe
The little guy
Scaled the fence"

"You said
He was cunning
And that you were watching
In suspense"
Another says

"That doesn't mean
Am trying to come to his defense"
The first speaker replies

"Well
I still can't believe
You stopped running"
The second speaker rasped
"I was tired and he was fast"
The first says
"It's because you are fat"
 The third laughs

"If you
Hungry bellied
Buffoons
Had brains
As big as my stomach size"
The first says
"Then maybe
You wouldn't have all gone
To chase his brother
On the other side

You left me on my own
I think it's clear
Am not a speedy bloke
You guys win
The trophy for the most genius
Idea spoke"
He laughs

"I don't see the joke"
The second warden
Responds to the tease
He sounds like
Authority
And the leader of the three

"You let him go too easily
For my liking
We'd better find him
Or I'll give you a hiding
So severe
You'll be lucky to be left alive"

"Yes sir"
The other says
"Am just following orders
As normal
And as you please
I've got no problem
With the lovers
I've just got needs
And a mouth to feed

Sometimes I feel
Sad for them
I just want to act right
At times
I get the feeling
That we are the bad guys"

"We'll talk about
Your commitment
After we've got the kid
Back to the metropolis"
The leader hisses

"An then we will
See about your..."
He pauses
"Hey
What's this?"

They're
Silent

The sound
Of a plastic bag rustling

Again silence

Whispers
Which again
Turn to nothing

Then
Footsteps
Crunching

Coming closer

Approaching

They stop close

A large hand grabs
Eugene by the throat

"I've got you
You little cockroach"

10. OMAR

The mean team
Of wardens
Had caught him
And showed no care
For his scream
Eugene looked
To the large man for help
But
He was nowhere to be seen

Missing
Gone
From behind
The tree where
He was hiding in fright
With no one to impede
The wardens proceed
To ride with their spite

"I told you we would find him"
One of them says
As he strides into sight with jive
"Only thing left to decide
Is do we return him dead or alive"

A menacing grin
Strung across his dirty skin
And slim face
One round warden
One trim
One tall string
Thin frame

The leader is the trim one
Grim features
Teeth sharp
His rough ached palm
Pinning
Eugene to the tree's bark

"Mortimer said
He wants him back
With gas in his lungs"
He snarls
"But wouldn't expect
We return
The young pest
Without having some fun"

And with that
He cocks
His arm back

And
Buff
He punches Eugene
In the stomach lower
Which causes him to puff
Clutch his gut
And double over

They wrestle him to the floor
And tie
His hands with a rope noose
He struggles
One hand
Broke loose
But they were too strong
It was no use

"Keep still
Ya little worm"
The slim one says
Using his foot
To rough him up
They hold him face down
Until the rope is tight enough
Then they stand him up

Another clenched fist
Takes flight
Towards his face
Eugene closes his eyes
Just before it struck
He
Couldn't look

And then

Cluck!!!

What sounds
Like a baseball
Being struck

But
Eugene is untouched
He opens his eyes
To look

And sees
The leader of the wardens
Toppling like falling timber
He crashes to the floor face first
And starts to snore
And whimper

The other wardens
Spin round
To find
Themselves
Looking up at the large man

With the axe cocked
Like a bat
Rusted blade side
In his hand

"Who on earth are you?"
The fat warden asks surprised
"Am the voice of the oppressed"
The giant-sized man replies

He delivers two precise swipes
And
As the axe handle
Impacts on cheeks
They topple to the grass
And both fall fast asleep

Birds leave the trees
Startled by the reverberation
The man in victory stance
Using the back of his hand
To wipe his perspiration

"You okay kid?"
He says
As he unties Eugene's hands
From the knot that they're placed in
"Am fine"
Eugene says
"Am just happy
You found me before they did"

"My names Omar"
The man says
Placing his
Hand forward
For Eugene to shake it
He takes it and tells
Omar
What his name is

"Those wardens were
Talking about someone
Escaping from an estate
Was that you?"
He says plain
Eugene's face exclaimed
That he is unsure whether to take the claim

Bird songs
Heard
Through
Thrusting branches
Bustling

Eugene's heart busting to speak
But
How could he trust him?

"If that
 Was you
They won't stop coming after you
Until they capture you
And
Any other unfortunate fool
That you're with
They'll capture too
And… that's the truth"

A steel glazed look
Falls over his face
Whilst his speech is fading
A look as if he had
Just come into a realisation

"Well kid
Good luck"
He says
As if
In a sudden hurry
"I have to go
Before
Floods of
These rookie
Bullies come
Looking for
Me"

He puts his axe on his shoulder
Steps to Eugene
And again
Shakes his hand
He turns and steps
To rush towards the bush
Into the woodland

"They want to kill all lovers"
Eugene replies
With words hurled
"We think they're planning
Genocide
I have to try and warn the world
Before it's too late"

Omar stops in his tracks
Looks back
As if studying Eugene's face
"Then the One has brought us together"
He says
"We have to make moves in haste

You cannot survive alone
I'll try and keep you safe but
We have to leave now
Before these wardens wake up"

11. DRIVE

"Come on kid keep up"

Eugene tries to keep pace
With Omar's wide strides
But his failure
Is due to his awe
Of the regalia
And the scale
Of the beauties in nature

He had forgotten how it was

Filled with life
Butterflies flutter by
And
Leaves
Lots of leaves
Like people
So many different types

Some green some red
Some brown some golden yellow
Some holding tight
To their branches
Where others had let go
And were dancing with the breeze

The dead still bringing life
To its woodland home
The constant buzz
Of insects and bugs
Reminding him that
No one is ever alone

They move quickly
Through thick prickly shrubs
Then cut and turn
Racing
Past
Floral decorations
There is no easy path
To their destination

After some time of navigating
Through the woodland
In covert mode
They arrive at a truck
Hidden behind a bush
Next to a dirt road

An old dusty brown
Rusted
Pickup truck

Is sat there waiting
And by Eugene's
Estimation
It's the product of
Major restoration

Blue dented doors
A crumpled sunk in bumper
And at the front
Broken lamps
The rear
Is filled with
Large branches
Sticks
Chopped logs and planks

"Get in"
Omar commands
Like
He's sending
Orders to bold troops
Eugene opens the door
Which releases
The scent
Of perfume
And old boots

He steps into
The passenger side
Of the cock pit
Expecting
It to be as
Bust as the crust
But it's the opposite

Red plush leather seats
The dashboard neat
And dressed with flair too
There's a metallic green love heart
Medallion
Dangling from the rear view

Omar jumps in

Eugene's
Expression
As if he didn't
Know which
Words to utter
"What's up?"
Omar asks
"Has no one ever told you
Never judge a truck
By its cover"
He laughs

"Our leader says we should
Work on purifying our insides
Before the visible
And am the type
To take that spiritual
Message into the literal"

Eugene nods

"He taught us that
If we want to
Rid the world
Of its ills
And repel hurt
We have to go within
And clean
The dirt within ourselves first"

He puts the key in the ignition
And revs
It purrs with no delay in the start
"It might not be physically attractive"
He grins
"But boy
Do you fall in love
With its heart"

He revs it again
And holds
Whilst lifting the clutch
Until the biting
He drops
The hand-break
The truck thrusts
And busts
From behind the bush
Where it was hiding

Dust flying behind them
The screech of the tires

Scooot!

He wrestles with the wheel
To keep it straight
Then they're on route

The drive is smooth

"Where are we going?"
Eugene asks
Whilst looking out of the window
At the green scenes
Squinting because of the suns light
Glinting
Through the windscreen

"Well
When the wardens
Came for lovers"
Omar says
In his husky tune
That had lost its play

"They planned to get us all
But a lucky few
Got away

And by the Ones praise
And reverence
We made our way to the woods
And have been hiding there
In a small settlement
Ever since
You will be safe
With us there"
He says
"We have been
Living there
In peace
For the last
Few years"
He claims

"There are
About a hundred of us
Mostly lovers
But also
Some other faculties

You see
Real lovers
Perceive all
Human beings
To be one family"

"Others?"
Eugene asks
Interrupting
Omar's speech
"Yep"
Omar nods
"Putting lovers
In estates
Was just
The first degree for them
Eventually
Undesirables
Became a term
For anyone
Who doesn't
Agree with them

It's all about control"
He tuts

"Lovers are
The enemy now
Because it's hard to control
People who take their morality
From a heavenly power

Dean Jiles
What a mean pile
Of greasy slob
Both him and his squad

I don't think
He'll stop
His merciless
Plot
Until
Every sorry sod's
Subservient
And he's worshipped as God"

Eugene is
Listening purposefully

"I'll stop him"
He bursts
Terse
Immersed in Omar's words
His smile reversed
Riling
At the mere mention of Dean Jiles

Omar laughs
"Stop him?
You?
Certainly not
Most of his orders
Come from the other
Side of the world
Where he works from a locked box room
And only ever surfaces
To give sermons
To his close servants
And a closed circle of yobs

No one ever gets close

I understand your anger"
Omar says
"And overstand your amplitude
But anger
Is a good way to choose
If you plan to lose"

"You'd be angry too"
Eugene says
"If you knew
What they've put
Me and my family through"

"Ay kid"
Omar soothes
"You're not the only dude
They've screwed

They split my family too
I don't
Even know if they're alive
The last time I spoke
To my wife
She was kicking
And screaming
For life"
He pauses

"I was walking
Home in the snow
After a quiet
Night shift
Whilst on the phone to her
When she
Opened the door to some guys

I heard the voice of an official
There was some scuffling
And then she screamed
The line went silent
So
I sprinted to catch them at the scene

But
By the time I got there
It was too late
She was gone
She was pregnant
With our son"
Omar's face
Turned to glum

"Some of the neighbours
Stated
She was
Probably taken
To an estate
Where they claim
That lovers
Volunteer
For work and
Re-education

With that
Information
I knew they'd
Likely come for
Me next
But my reflex
Was to search
For her
In every creek and recess

I became depressed
A lonely wanderer
Searching
The forbidden
Standing
Outside
Those estate prisons
Hoping
To spot her within

Staying hidden
Praying
Switching between
Estates
And because I couldn't
Find her
I was losing
The will for living

I wanted to
End it all
I felt like there was
No escape
I was low
And when old Laith
Found me
I was close to breaking"

"Old Laith?"
Eugene asks
"That's the name
Of our teacher"
Omar adds
"The one who founded
The settlement
The chief
Our leader

When he found me
He said
My heart was
Covered with sorrow
As thick as leather
He took me in
With a smile and told me
Tomorrow will be better

Never have
I felt such love
From a stranger
True lovers care
Never have
I felt more away from danger
So
I'll take you there

They'll be happy
To receive a new face
Well
All except Kamari
He won't be happy
But ignore whatever that
Dude says"

"Kamari?"
Eugene asks

"Yea
Kamari"
Omar replies
With every new arrival
He gets stressed out
One time he....
Wait…"
Omar pauses
"That wasn't there when I left out"

12. DON'T WORRY

Omar frowns
As his gaze
Stretches far down the road
Looking
As a distant dot emerges

"Patrol car
Up ahead"
He says
"I think they're conducting
Stop and searches"

"Turn around"
Eugene says

"No chance"
Omar replies
"They've probably spotted us
They use binoculars
Any wrong move now
And they'll be onto us

There's no way on earth
We could out run them in this
This baby was built for beauty
It wasn't made to be swift

Well kid
It was nice meeting you"
Omar's sigh
A despairing show
Then he turns
To see
Eugene squeezing
Himself through
The sliding rear window

He gets
Stuck
But
A hard push
From Omar
Helps him through
He falls into
The cargo bed
Onto the logs
But loses a shoe

He wiggles into a gap
Between freshly cut
Pieces of hefty wood
Then covers himself
With a hand full
Of branches
The best he could

He pulls
A bunch over his face
Like a hood
A complete disguise
And
Between
The leaves
Of the branches
That he'd applied
He could see the skies

"Don't worry"
Omar calls
"I always carry
My old ID papers
So providing they
Don't chase up on them
There'll be no danger"

Eugene hears
The thud of
The window shutting
As Omar slides it closed
And
The grim
Grumbling of engines
Mumbling
As they drive in close

They join a queue
Of two or three other cars
That are being checked
The truck slowly crawls forward
As they wait to be inspected

The voice of a warden
Ordering
Makes Eugene's heart tremor
"Park over there"
She states
In a tempered
Tenor of hard terror

He feels the truck
Pull to the side of the road
For the intended encroach
And then
Hears spit splat onto the floors
As wardens make
An unfriendly approach

"What seems to be
The problem mam"
Omar initiates the conversation
"Vehicle permission
And travel papers"
The warden says
Her voice strong and impatient

One warden
Stands by the driver's side
Checking the papers
That she'd been given
Another
Starts searching
Through the logs
Near to where Eugene is hidden

He begins flinging
Planks of wood
Slinging logs
And
Coming close
Eugene froze
As some of
The wood's dust
Whooshes
Up his nose

Feeling the heat
He lay still
Between
Cut pieces of tree
He squeezes
His nostrils together
To impede
His need to sneeze

"We're on the seek for
An escapee"
Says the warden
Who is neighbouring Omar
Whilst
The other warden
Is rummaging
The load
Slowly tapering closer

"Yea"
The other
Warden says
In a ruff scraping voice
Just a breath away
"The pesky
Little sneaker escaped
From the Cedar Estate
Yesterday"

Eugene
Holding still
Holding breath
Tensed
Holding clenched fist
And toes
As defense
Against being sensed

"Sorry
I've not seen anyone so far"
Replies Omar
His tone marched over
The faint sounds of Jupiter
By Mozart
Playing
From the patrol car

Barp barp barp

The sound of the patrol cars
Radio alarm
Begins blaring in the distance

"Wardens attacked
In the Woods
West region
Boy seen
In need of assistance"

Said a voice that came exploding
Over their radio
The warden searching
Turns away
Just as he moves the branch
That leaves Eugene's
Shaken looking face exposed

They both race towards their vehicle
In a fluster
To respond to the call
Their footsteps
Rushing away but then
One of them stalls

Those same footsteps
Track back toward the truck
The pace is fast
"Oi you"
The warden says
Tapping the glass
"I forgot to give your papers back"

"Thanks"
Omar says
In response
To the honest cue
"Hold on a minute"
The warden says
"Who's that shoe belong to?"

Eugene
Squirms as his
Need to sneeze gets stronger
His face scrunches into a pose
He couldn't hold his nose any longer

"Ha Chuuuu"

The biggest
And loudest
Sneeze
That he had ever done
Thrashes
Through the truck
And stuns
Everyone

"The boy is here
The boy is here"
The excited warden yelps quick

"Brace yourself kid"
Omar yells
The engine starts
And he belts it

The spinning wheels
Scream
As the truck skids
And blasts again
Eugene sits
Up swiftly and sees
The warden
Sprinting after them

Her helmet flings
Into the wind
Her brown hair blowing
Vicious
Limbs swinging
Vigorously
Her face full of bitterness

The patrol car
Fires up
And jets
Full speed toward
It pulls up beside
The chasing warden
Who gets on board

The wardens give chase
Siren's thumping
Dust erupting
Disrupting the nirvana
The speed of the pursuit
Is like cheetah hunting impala

Omar's
Fully on the gas
But still
The gap's closing fast
Eugene's holding on with all his might
As they dash

"They're going to catch us
They're getting closer"
Eugene shouts to Omar
"Lighten the load"
Omar howls
"Throw those logs over"

Eugene hoists logs
That bounce
And roll
Like barrels
As he deploys them
The patrol car
Turning
And swerving
To avoid them

"It's no use"
Eugene shouts
"They're still
Gaining on us fast"
"Release the latch"
Omar screams
"The black safety catch
At the back"

Eugene spots
The black safety catch
That would open
The frail rattily tail gate
And send all
The logs and planks
Hurtling into a spate

He stands up
Straight
The wind
Rocking him
As he strides
And the bumps of the ride
Nearly
Sends him flying
Over the side

He keeps his balance
Then checks
The warden's car progressing
Both wardens with vexed look
Their eyes red
With raw aggression

He pulls the safety catch
The tailgate
Flings open
The warden's faces
Change to fear
As sticks
Planks
And logs
Go gushing out of the rear

The patrol car swings
Switching and swishing
Dodging to miss sticks
But they're hit by a log
Which sends them veering
Into a ditch

Screech

Smash

Smoking

Eugene makes his way
To the front of the truck
From off the wagon
He squeezes through
The window
And falls back into the cabin

"That's enough action for one day"
Eugene tiredly asserts
"Well done kid"
 Omar says
"Team work made the dream work"

13. SETTLEMENT

An hour or so of
Driving in near silence
Had passed
Since their
Slide in
With those feared tyrants
Now
They are
Both in thought
The last time
They had spoken
Was a few miles back
Whilst driving
Around an island

Sun
Shining behind them

"Are we lost?"
Eugene had asked
As they circled
A roundabout
For the third cross
"Just making sure we haven't got a tail"
Omar says as he turns off

"We've been living free
To a degree
While others
Are in estate prisons
The key to our success
Has been
Making sure that we stay hidden"

They were definitely well hidden
Eugene thought
As they drove off road
Through a bush
Onto a bumpy
Country track
The sound of crumbling
Stones under the tires
Crunch and crack

They drive
Through grassy fields
Where singing birds
Swim skies like open seas
And a free-flowing breeze
Waves through
The branches
Of the trees

Through a valley
Under a bridge
Across a meadow
Then back onto road
And as they approach a
Stretch of woodland
They slow

They park the truck
Behind a bush
Near the entrance
Of the wood
"Okay" Omar says
"We do the rest on foot"

Whilst clambering
Out of the truck
He grabs the medallion
From the mirror
Places it over his neck
Light shimmers
Off its sterling silver

He calls to his companion
"Come on kid
Let's get moving"
But Eugene is struck by the beauty
He's musing

They enter
Through an arbor arch way
Made of large
Beautifully carved stakes
Decorated
With gold paint
And an engraving
On its frame
'All are in need of One
One is in need of none'
It says

Violet coloured
Grape hyacinths
And bluebell flowers
Lined
The path either side of it
As if desiring
To rise above
The run
And
Dandelion weeds
Swaying
Moving
With the lightest breeze
But never breaking
They stand strong
Looking like the sun

The sun
Whose
Light
Illuminates
The pathway
Which is made of
Flattened grass blades
And dead leaves
That are
Trodden
Into a trail
Leading
A way into
The boscage
With
Moss draping
Across the landscape
Primrose flowers
Mandrake
And other plants
Make up the terrain

Omar leads the way
Down a path which breaks
Into lanes
Like a maze
They step over roots
That look
Like veins

Leaves
Fall
Like rain

The wood opens
Out onto a meadow
Where an old
Bungalow stands ahead
Alone
The wind blowing melody
Whilst their footsteps
Tread the metronome

"The bungalow's my place"
Omar says
As they approach it
"It's an outpost mostly
I was chosen to host it"

It had an old brown door
White stone walls and a black patched
Thatch roof
Detached from the surrounding
It stood there aloof

"That's only one house"
Eugene complains
"Where are all the people
You said there was a
Community
That had escaped the
Grip's evil"

They swished through
The grass
Which came up
Past Eugene's waist
Until they came to the ledge
Of the pass
Where Omar waits

For Eugene
Whose stride was now a dally
"The settlement"
Omar states
Pointing down into a valley
Eugene rushes
To look over the side
Excited to take the sight in
"Wow"
He exclaims
Amazed
His eyes widen

The site from that height
Strikes Eugene
Like a cannon
The settlement was
Even more beautiful than
He'd imagined

There are wooden
Huts and cabins
Either side of a flowing river
Flowers growing everywhere
Too many
People pottering around to figure

Fishermen sitting
On a bridge
Filling
Wicker baskets with their catch
And people farming gardens
With vegetable patches attached

A pageant of
Cherry blossom petals
Whirling
And swirling into patterns
Children play
Laughing
Jumping to try and catch them

Crowing
Chickens roaming
And cows
Mowing the turf
Boats on the river
That quiver
Bobbing the surface

"Let's go meet Laith"
Omar says
And with quick pace
He takes a rope
That's fixed to a stake
And begins to abseil the cliff face

Which activates a pulley system
A wooden platform lifts up as he goes down
It reaches up to Eugene
As Omar touches the ground

"You know what to do" he shouts

Eugene carefully mounts the platform
Which wobbles as he stands on it
It take him to the ground
And they head towards the hamlet

As they reach in
They meet a girl
With brown skin and sky blue eyes
She gives them greetings
"Evening Omar
Where you been?
Who's the new guy?"

They walk past huts
As people wave from door steps
And windows
They continue over the bridge
A fisherman's smile and wink shows

Children stop their play
And begin running around
Eugene's legs
Singing
"A new boy
Omar brought a new boy"
Whilst tugging at his threads

"That's Laiths huts ahead"
Omar says
Eugene stops to see
A smaller hut
With a large flower garden
Which housed the blossom tree

It was at the heart of the settlement
They briskly walked towards it
And without knocking or calling
Omar opened up its door

14. LAITH'S HUT

Musk
As sweet as heavenly honey
A unique dressing of
Sweet smelling
Fresh and refreshing
Musk
Swept from the dwelling
And met them as they stepped in

A fragrance so
Fragrant they could nearly taste it
This is what Eugene imagined
Blessings to smell like

Inside
Natural light
Floods
Through clean curtain-less windows
Touching every surface
Which made the room
Glow
With golden warmth

The subtle crackle of logs
In a fireplace smoldering
But no smoke at all
The only aroma is
The potent lick of
Musk
A sweet-smelling musk

The inside of the hut
Seems
Much larger
Than the outside
Jars and pots filled with plants
Scattered around the hive

An oak armchair
A maple coloured wooden table
A cushioned wooden sofa
A tapestry of greys and blues

"Laith"
Omar calls
"Old Laith?"
Again he says
"Omar?"
Replied a gentle voice
Then from out of the pantry
Popped the friendly face of Laith

Grooved
Cinnamon skin
White beard
White shirt
A green and gold cape
The calm on his face
Says he isn't
Fazed by his old age
Or slow pace

"Is everything okay?"
He says
Bringing forward
His short frame
"Hello my boy"
He smiles
Noticing Eugene
"What's your name?"

Boom!

The door flings open
With such force
That it nearly
Breaks away from the door frame

A young man and woman
Come storming
Towards Laith
The man enraged

"His names Eugene"
The man states whilst
Scraping
His short black
Straightened hair
To clear his face
"He escaped from an estate
Yesterday
Father
He mustn't stay here"

He's tall
His face pimpled
His nose
Wrinkled up
His attitude
Hostile
"Kamari?"
Eugene whispers to Omar
Omar nods a smile

"Calm yourself down Kamari"
Laith says
Speaking with gracious speech
"I was just about to make a pot of tea
Please take a seat"

Kamari stares at Laith
His round face
Reeks
Of dismay and seethe
But Laith is at ease
With a smile that displays his teeth

Laith's eyebrows raise
Then
Kamari's change
To a frown
He looks back
At Eugene
And then he sits down
Slamming his hand
On the table

"Absolute foolishness
How can we remain hidden
When he's bringing in fugitives
This kids all over the news" he says

His voice is deep and strong
He picks up a remote and
Clicks the tv on

A bleach blond
News presenter
Is sat there
Centre screen
With hypnotic speech
And eyes that
Scream intensity

"In other news"
She says
Her face straight
No smile at all
"The hunt still continues
For a dangerous undesirable

We're joined
By chief warden Mortimer
Who's now
At the Cedar Estate
Mortimer
Please tell us the developments
In the case of this kid who escaped"

The screen cuts
To Mortimer
Who's stood
In front of the Cedar Estate gate
With wardens
Either side of him
All of them mean in face

"Well
We're doing all we can"
He says
"We've deployed
The Muscle
The best bounty hunters
In the land
And we're offering reward
For anyone who can bring
This young man
To our hands

We understand that
He may have
Assistance
But I must declare
That for those caught
With him
The punishment will be severe

Undesirables
They've brought menace to our society
So we offered them education
How do they repay it?
They throw it in our faces

We try to help these animals
But they can never be helped
They're a danger to the city
Themselves and everyone else"
He says

"This escape
Is proof that
They can't be trained
Or contained
So
We need
Another way to keep you safe
From their maim"

The screen splits to show scenes
Of firefighters
Fighting the flames
Of a burning building
Then another shot
Shows the remains

"Remember the time
Undesirables put bombs
In that store
For want of a war
And killed without a conscience
Or thought

You see
These ruthless monsters
They only ever want us to fall
We need a solution
To rid us of them
Once and for all"

The camera cuts
And pans to show
The squalor of an estate
With inhabitants
Looking broken
Downtrodden and debased

"It's evolution"
Mortimer says
"They are not equal
They're not even people
But more akin to beast
Weasels
Beetles

Or any other pest
Or germ impersonation
This type of infestation
Should be faced
With extermination"

The camera switches to
A close up
Of his eyes
The windows to a soul
Filled with arrogance and pride

"We have decided
To make sure
That no more mistakes follow
By beginning the cleansing
Of the Cedar Estate tomorrow

They might call themselves lovers
But trust us
They're all the same
Undesirable
Unpleasant
Undeserved of a name"

"Thank you
Mortimer
And again
The main news" The presenter says
As the screen displays a sketch of Lewis
"This morning
The first escapee was caught and has been executed

It came after him and his brother
Escaped
And hunters searched daylong
He was captured and killed
But for Eugene
The search goes on"

"Up next"
She says
As the exit music
Strikes the passage
"Programming on
Why undesirables
Are the worst type of savage
And how we can manage them"

She shuffles her paper stack
"That's enough of that"
Laith says
And the screen is switched to black

15. FATE

The room is quiet

Laith is stood holding remote
Kamari still sat in his place
Eugene standing still
Next to Omar
Tears streaming down Eugene's face

"Lewis"
He whispers
As an ocean forms
Over his eye balls
And tears fall
From his chin
And slowly soak
Into the pine floor

"We need to get him away from here"
Kamari pelts at Omar's self
"No
We need to keep him close"
Omar says
"This kid right here
 Needs our help"

"Why were you even
In that area?"
Kamari asks Omar
Whilst scouting
The subtle
Strife in him
"You've
Endangered our lives
Bringing him here
Were you looking for your wife again?"

"You leave my wife out of this"
Omar counters quick
In his loudest pitch
Shouting
With clenched fist
Spouting
Ready to bout
Clout or hit

"You're a fool"
Kamari says
"An utter idiot"
He makes a stance
"If they trace him here
They'll throw us all straight
Into one of those camps"

Omar locks eyes with Kamari
Delivering him a death stare
"I found the kid alone"
He blares
"Do you expect me
To have just have left him there?"

"We must keep the settlement
Safe at all costs"
Kamari replies
As he walks closer
"We can't take any chances
Am going to hand him over"

Kamari goes to grab Eugene
But Omar blocks his way
He blocks him with his body
"You won't lay a finger on him"
He says

"I implore you to control yourselves"
Laith demands
In a stern but tender tone
"Please remember
He's our guest
We must make him feel at home

We must use words
To build" he adds
"Because
Words behave like bricks
When thrown around
They can break hearts
Which are sometimes
Hard to fix

Kind words are best here"
He assures
With a positively
Charged demeanor
"Harsh words
Don't reflect their target
They're a reflection of their speaker"

Omar and Kamari calm
Like students
Under a teacher
Laith defused the two
Disputing
With the prudence of a preacher

"Take a seat here my boy"
Laith pats the arm chair
To welcome him

"You probably
Haven't eaten
In days"
Your limbs
Are incredibly thin"

"Am sorry about your brother"
He says
As he goes into the pantry
And takes out a tray of snacks to eat
But Eugene walks past him
Looking downcast
And beat

He walks towards the door
With tired limbs
And a passive face
"Sorry"
He says
"I must get to the city
Straight away
I cannot stay

He opens the door
And the sound of
The children playing
Burst into scene
The calm sound of the river
The breeze
Serene

"They killed my brother"
Eugene says
With anger loaded in
Stressed words
"I have to alert the lovers
Before anyone else gets hurt"

"Alert the lovers?"
Laith questions
"We are the lovers"
He smiles
"Who else did you want to warn?
We're the only ones left
My child

I mean
There are still a few lovers in the city
Hidden among the city folk
But they're in no position
To make the difference that you hope

Most lovers are in estates
The rest of us are here in hiding
Surviving off nature
Striving on the Ones providing

Besides
Did you think to go by yourself?"

"We're born alone
We die alone"
Eugene replies
"I don't need any help"

"Born alone
Die alone?"
Laith frowns
"Well that there's not true
No one is ever born alone"
He steps closer
"Am sure your mother was there too

And to die alone
I think you maybe forget
The angel of death my boy?
Humans were made to connect
Those who fail to accept help
Are often left with major regrets"

Laith takes a step over to some lilies
That are growing from a pot
He takes a watering can
And starts to pour water on the top
"Do you think you got here by yourself?
Without the Ones help and guidance"
He says
"Those subtle signs placed
Along your way
In places where you could find them

Think back to your journey my boy
You'll find nothing is disjointed
Everything has happened only
To bring you to this point

There are
No coincidences
Think back and you will see
The One has been clearing
Your path
To bring you
To me

All for me to tell you this

The lone ranger
Always thinks
He can do things on his own
But the seed needs soil
Water and light to be grown

And the more time
Care and love
We share
The stronger it will get
Everything needs everything
My boy
So don't you forget

Nothing is independent
Nothing except the One
All are in need of Him
He's the only in need of none"

"There's no one else to warn"
The woman says
Her voice came lancing through
"We all know what they're planning
But what else can we do?"

It was the lady
That Kamari came with
She was sat cross legged
In a chair
She was sat
So quietly
They all had
Forgotten she was there

She had taken roost
In the corner of the room
Next to the window
Where a small
Opening is
Letting the breeze
Blow in slow
And is
Wafting her long
Jet black hair into
A flow
Lifting it up from her woolen
Colour filled poncho

Pecan brown skin
Thin
She wears a dark green beret hat
Black beaded bangles on her wrists
Her hands folded in her lap

She stands up with grace
Walks over to Laith
A brave face equipped
She takes a cup from the tray
That he had
And slowly takes a sip

Her green eyes
Locked on Eugene
There's a toughness in her vibe
Purpose in her movements
A sadness deep inside

"The city folk"
She grunts
"They're the ones
Who need waking up
They're stuck under a spell
Allowing Dean Jiles
To undertake this muck

He's been brainwashing
Them for years
To make them think all lovers are evil
And deceitful
When the opposite is indeed true

Everyday
They show us in the negative
On their screens
And now the city folk are ready
To get rid of us by any means"

"They'll stop at nothing
For complete control"
Kamari says softly
His snarling face
Had swapped
To a calmer state
A softy

"My father Laith
Left the city
After seeing the pattern in
How they think
He brought us here
We've made it home and have
Been growing ever since

Those people out there
Have made it into what it is today
And I'll do anything I can
To keep them all safe"

"But
We have to do something
To help the others"
Eugene says
"You're living a life of comfort
While other lovers
Live in terror
Your settlement is a treasure
But you can't hide
Here forever"

"The boy's right"
Laith agrees
"Certainly
It's our purpose to respond
For
Those who help others
Are true servants of the One

I've always thought
If we could get ourselves on
Their screens
During peak time for
Entertainment
And make a statement
We could maybe
Wake some people
To this abasement"

"It's not like we can
Just waltz into
A screening room
And book ourselves a slot"
Kamari says
"If we can get into the city"
Laith returns
"I don't see why not"

He perches
On a chair
Lays back
Whilst
Stroking
His bushy
White beard
His eyes steer
In Omar's direction as if
Looking for ideas

"I know a route in"
Omar says
"It's an underground
Connection
When I was loose
I would use it
To sneak in and out of the city
Without detection"

"There're probably
Swarms
Of wardens patrolling
That building"
Kamari says
"They're not likely
To ignore
Any shifty looking lovers
Trying to walk in through
Their doors"

"Of course
But
Anika here is like a wizard"
Laith says
"She's stacked
With computer wisdom
Am sure if she could
Get close enough
She could hack into their system
Hijacking their signal?"

His voice takes a suggestive tone
"Broadcasting us live
Into every single home?"

She smiles and nods
"Piece of cake
I'll get us on
I could override their system
But it wouldn't be for long"

"Even just a minute
At the right time
Would be enough"
Laith says
"To break this blind acceptance
And wake some of them up"

He turns to Eugene
And asks him
"What do you think?
Still want to go alone?
Or could we include you in
The team as the capstone

Look around my boy
This is fate
The Ones plan
Who else could gather such a group
This is much too big for one man"

Eugene walks out of the door
Then pauses
As if deciding

He steps back inside
And then closes the door behind him

"That settles it"
Laith says excitedly
He leaps forward quickly
"Have something to eat
Change your clothes
Tonight
You leave for the city"

16. THE CITY

The sky is dark
Heavy
Clouds
Like giant carts
Drop
Tiny darts of rain
Onto the trucks top

The climate is declining into minuses

Between the clouds
The brightest stars
Shining like
Diamonds
Guiding
Through the
Blinding darkness
A picture of the finest art

Omar's driving
Eugene's slumped
Beside him
He sighs
Hard
His crying eyes
Showing
Signs of a pining heart

"Sorry about your brother kid"
Omar says
Shaking his head
With the kind remark

"It's okay"
Eugene replies
Wiping his eyes
"I just can't believe…
He's dead"

"Well
He died a martyr
Which means
His soul resides
In the finest part
Of the highest parlor"
Omar says

Trying to harness
Comforting words
To revive his partners
Fighting spark

Eugene
Looks back
Into the cargo bed
Where
Anika and Kamari
Are
Anika checking
Her back pack
Kamari with
Folded arms

Staring into space
Rocking and bracing
Bopping with the terrain
Neither fazed
By the spots of rain
Dotting their faces

Eugene sights that
Kamari's dark eyes
Are hiding scars
"His whole family were taken"
Omar says

"Just him and his father
Survived
It grates him
And grinds him hard
He blames himself
For not being there
Now he lives his
Whole life on guard

That's why I shouldn't
Listen to
The words
He places in his passion
Words are just words
The truth
Shows in his action"

"What happened?"
Eugene asks
"The muscle"
Omar answers
"When it comes to hunting
Those two guys
Take the standard"

"Heavy handed
Brutes"
He says
His face displayed
The anger
"If I could get my hands on them
I'd show them both some manners"

The truck stops moving
They disembark
And take flight
All following
Omar through
The woods
Toward the
City's lights

They stop by
A stream
After
Coasting
Through the night
They drop onto
Its bank
Close to an
Open sewage pipe

It's oozing fluid
Spewing gunk
A fowl
Ejection
"Lady and gentlemen"
Omar says
"I present
The underground connection"

The stomach wrenching
Stench
Coerced
Them to
Clench their noses
With faces showing 'err'
"Right then"
Omar smiles
Looking into the pipe
"Which one of you is going first?"

"You mean to say
You want us
To go in there?"
Kamari asks
"Well
It's the only safe way
Into the city"
Omar laughs

"No chance"
Kamari blurts
"No sir
Not me" he says
Eugene moves him aside
And steps into the pipe
To lead the way

Omar lights a torch
"Let's steps in"
He grins
His voice echoing
Through the pipe
"The things we do for love" he sings

Anika shadows after
Leaving Kamari on his own
Blue
But after realising
He's alone
He decides to follow suit

Treading past
Rotting goo
They slog it through
The gutter
Mutters and murmurs are heard
But not a word is uttered

For half a mile
In single file
Inside the concrete cylinder
Avoiding waste and similar
By staying by the perimeter

Above them
Are steel sewage grates
Where rays of light
Descend
Omar stops
Beneath one
And says
"This is where we end"

He grips its metal
Edging
Stretches himself
To look outside
"All clear" he calls
Then he slides
The grate aside

Gallantly
He pulls himself up and out
Into an
Alleyway
Then offers
Down a helping hand
Eugene grabs
Without delay

Omar pulls him
Up and out
He dusts his clothes
And stands bold
Then Eugene
Helps Omar
To pull the others two out
The manhole

They check the alley
Then scurry
Up a cat ladder
Onto a roof
Then creep
Towards
The edge
And look out at the city
In its truth

A dazzling sight
Every premise
Fashioning
Fabulous lights
Like
Precious gems
Extravagant buildings
Sky scrapers
And mighty edifices
The luminesce
Hiding the blemishes of the city

Horns from
Slowly moving traffic blare
Affluence portrayed through
The prosperous postures
Of people passing
Strolling towards the fair

Giant screens
On every corner
Playing recordings
Of Dean Jiles
Talking
His storm like
Voice soaring
Over loud speakers
Squawking

His talk is
About the importance
Of following orders
And reporting
Any acts of love
That are not directed
Towards him

Dark hair
Side parting
Clean shaven
Serious face
His classic
Acid red
Seven-fold tie
Fastened
Neatly in place

One of his eyes
Permanently closed
And protruding
Like a grape
The other
Green and seems to
Track and trace
Any soul it makes contact with

Omar points to a building
Made of mirrors
It's pyramid shaped
"That's the media building"
He says
"Where most of the
Broadcasts are made"

"If we can get close enough"
Anika says
"We could
Cut their signal
And put you on
We could
Broadcast you
Nationwide
But
Like I said
It wouldn't be for long"

"You make it sound
Straight forward"
Kamari interrupts with a tut
"With all those wardens
Down there
How do you suppose
We get close enough?"

"We could do it"
Eugene asserts
Seeming quite certain
Urging
"We just need them to disperse
We just need to avert them
With a diversion"

Omar leaps up
And spurts
Towards the ladder
In a gust
"If a diversions
What you need"
He huffs
"Then leave it to us

Kamari
Come with me
I think we should take a cruise
You two
Keep watch from the roof but
Be ready to make your move

We'll pull them away from the building
And thrill them with a trick of mine
But as soon as you go live
They'll come back and
You'll have little time"

"Get your message
Straight
And then
Get away"
Kamari warns
Harshly
"We wouldn't want
Any harm to come of you"
His remark
Slightly sarky

"Remember
Team work
Makes the dream work"
Omar adds
His speech firm
Readying to descend
The ladder
He goes down in reverse

Ting ting ting

The sound
Of footsteps
As they climb down
Then the sound
Of their whispered
Arguments
Are heard from the ground

They appear at the front
Of the building
Omar leading
His head bowed
Eugene tries
To track them
But they disappear into the crowd

Eugene and Anika
Watch the people passing
From their rooftop perspective
Everyone
In fancy clothing
But all smiles
Neglected

"Beautiful isn't it?"
Anika says
Eugene traces her gaze
To see where her vision sits
"What is?" he asks
"The city"
She continues
"Ever since the eviction
I've been missing it

My parents helped build the broadcast system
Helped the city to improve and such
But when Dean Jiles came to power
They became lovers who knew too much

The conniver
He applied
A no survivors order on my family
And the wardens managed
To capture them all
Except me

My parents forced me to hide
So I hid
In the waste
Where I watched them
Bring both my parents
To their fate

How did we get to this point?"
She says
"What an awful game
Where some are taught
That they are better than others
When underneath
We're all the same"

"My father was arrested in secret"
Eugene says
"And taken for speaking
About the One with pride
My family think he's been killed
But I have hopes that he's still alive

It's insane"
He states
"The condition
Of the lovers
Are hideous
Whilst the city folk
Are
Living life
In luxury
Oblivious"

"After all that's happening"
Anika sighs
All the pain and the groan
"I still just want to come back home"

17. YOU'RE LIVE

Beep beep beeeeep

The sudden sound of
Horns honking
Takes their attention
Towards
The media building
Where two cars
Are doing
Donuts
On the road
Wheel's screeching
And squealing

"It's Omar and Kamari"
Eugene shrieks
With excited face
Both their heads
Poking out of
Open windows
Taunting the wardens
Inviting chase

Angry wardens spill
Out of the gates
And race to
Fill patrol cars
The pair go in opposite directions
Kamari
Then Omar

"They've taken the bait"
Eugene says
As the warden's chase
The duo
"Let's do what
We came to do"
Anika says
"Let's go"

Ducking and diving
Eugene and Anika
Navigate
Through alleyways
At thrilling pace
Hopping walls
And fences
Until they reach the
Media buildings gates

Eugene takes steps
Towards it
"Wait"
Anika whispers
Pulling him
Behind a statue
Of Dean Jiles
Narrowly
Saving him from
Being found
By a warden
Patrolling the grounds

She pulls him down
To where she's crouching
And takes out a laptop
Her fingers engage
"No need to get any closer"
She says
"I think we're in range"

She starts tapping
Squinting
And mumbling numbers
Relentlessly
"Got it" she says
Before slamming down the enter key

Which sends all screens
Into a buzzing
Fuzzing
White noise
"Ready when you are"
Anika says
Whilst getting
The camera poised

"I don't know what to say"
Eugene stutters
Looking unnerved
And numb
"Focus on
Giving them
Your heart"
Anika smiles
"And the words will come"

Eugene closes
His eyes calmly
Thinking of all the harm
They've faced
Before being interrupted by
The sound of
A car crashing
Not so far away

"Sorry to break
Your meditation"
Anika states
But we haven't got
Time to waste"
"Okay am ready"
Eugene nods
She presses a button
"You're live"
She says

Screens far and wide
Show a close up
Of Eugene's face
People in their homes
And on the streets
Stop
And watch
Amazed

People in the city
People in estates
People in the settlement
Locked in
To hear his case

"I am not afraid anymore"

He says
His eyes raise from the floor
Until his gaze reaches dead centre lens
His eyes displaying bite
Eyes that say despite
The tyranny
There's still the will to fight

"Fear has caused
Our silence
And given
Our power to
Ruling forces
Our thoughts
Forbidden
Our love hidden
Our talk stricken with rigor mortis
They've taught
You to fear us
And
Taught us
That we're naught
Plus
They told you they would reform us
But their plan is to make us corpses"
He says

"We were
Your neighbours
Your retailers
Your doctors
And your tailors
You knew we weren't
Dangerous
But held your statement
When they came
To take us

Too afraid to say
In case it took you out
Your comfort

To speak up
Felt like a stunt
But could have saved us
From the shunt

Whilst you sit at home
And watch station
Upon station
Of entertainment
They have been
Painstakingly
Planning our enslavement
And erasure

I am done with
Being afraid"
He says
"Fear is the reason
They have us engulfed
In this state
We are weak
And have become
Like
Sheep following wolves

It's the reason why
We turn a blind eye
When they divide us and tell us lies
We have to wake up
Because now they're planning
Genocide

They
Portray us as traitors
And make you hate us
It's trickery and deceit
Deliberately
Taking liberties and
History repeats

I broke free from an estate
And risked my life
To bring this message
You folk have to
Wake from sleep
Your silence
Is oppressive

Your ignorance
Is killing us
An awakening
Must soon ensue
Am asking you to
Stand up with us
Because
We are human too

We must break
This fear"
He says
"And overcome its slopes
Outside this fear is love
And with love
There is hope

Lovers
Wear your love on your sleeves
And also on your faces
Love shouldn't be hidden away
But displayed so all can take from it

Love is what binds us
It's what defines us
And ignites us
They want us divided
They loose
Control when we're united

Let's do what is right
Together
Despite the discomforts
That may befall
Let us call for lovers
To be freed
Once and for all

Dean Jiles
Plans to place the whole world
In his thrall
So
United we must stand
Or
Divided we will fall"

Smash!!

The camera dashes
Across the street
And brakes in half
Rendering all screens
To a buzzing
Leaving Eugene and Anika jarred

A large stone
Falls to the road
After being thrown
Hard
A warden with his throwing arm
Still finishing the motion
Was the star

His cold heart
Told
By the
Calm
In his
Expression
He progresses
Quickly
Towards the two
Aggression fueling his stepping

Within a second
He's in front of them
Mean
Speed and stature supreme
They try to run
But he leans
And captures Eugene

"Eugene"
 Anika calls
She lifts the laptop
And cracks it
On the wardens back
It snaps
With a crash
The warden
Turns to face her
He laughs

He
Lifts his big black boot
Cocks his leg back
And with a flash movement
He kicks and hits Anika
Who
Flies back into the statue

The force of the kick
Causes him to
Lose grip
Of Eugene
Who
Retreats and speeds
To help Anika to her feet
She rises
Coughing
Grasping her chest
She takes a breath
Gasping

She
Then launches
A blasting
Attack
Straight back at him

Roaring
Like a lioness
Her claws soaring
Towards
His eyes
He steps side to side
Dodging
Every blow she tries

And then
His weapon rises
And…
It gets her…

Her gasp
Long and deep
The terrain is not
Made to absorb pain
So her gasp echoes
Off the concrete

From one street
To another
Carrying
Into the far away

"Nooo"

Eugene cries
"Run"
Anika
Calmly says

She takes out a weapon
That was placed in her waist band
And gets the warden back
Both weapons fall from their hands

Then both bodies
Fall limp
As time seems to slow
Eugene rushes
And
Catches
Her head
Before it touched the road
Her eyes closing
Closed

"Anika!"

Eugene calls
"Don't worry"
She coughs
"Am okay"
"Anika!"
Eugene says again
But nothing more
Could she relay

She just lay
Next to the warden
Both
Dead

Silent

The only sound
Is from sirens
And
The heavy stamping boots
Of wardens approaching
From around the wall behind him

He stands up
Without panic
Managing to
Stay strong
And briskly walks
Into the alley
They had came from

Then he starts a jog
Which turns into a dash
Springing
Over the walls
And the fences
Until at last

He is back in that alleyway
Climbing into the manhole
Slugging through the black
Of the tunnel as blind as a mole

It seems like
Endless darkness
Until light at the end appears
Where he hears struggling
And grunting
Outside the tunnel
As he nears

There are
Two silhouettes
Tussling just outside the exit
And as he gets closer
He sees
One of them is Omar

Eugene quickens his step
His face wet and dripping with sweat
His tired legs tripping
To get to Omar
And help against the threat

He slips on the deck
And slides out of the pipe
Head first
Splashing into the stream
The sound causes Omar to turn

Taking advantage
The other man tries to grab him
But grabs
His medallion
Which pops off
And slings
Into the air
Like a coin
Then drops
Lost

Omar goes after it
In a flurry
Scurrying
On hands and knees
Searching through
The weeds
To retrieve
The missing piece

The man walks after him
His weapon stretches
Out of his leather vest
Ready to get Omar
Ready to put him to rest

Eugene
Scrambles out of the water
Tramples
Onto the bank
With anvil ankles
He finds a plank in
The brambles and
Untangles it
Handling it with both hands
He raises the plank towards
The star-spangled sky
The stars like candles
That hang
They illuminate the plank
He angles it above
The mans head
Eugene swings through
And…

CRACK!!

The bash
Sends the man collapsing down
Crashing into a bed of leaves
Which splash from the ground
Then sprinkle down like confetti pieces
They cover him like a sheet

Eugene peeps over him
Checking to see
If he's breathing
The sound that he's making
Says he isn't dead
Just heavy sleeping

"Who is this?"
Eugene asks

"Bounty hunter"
Omar says
Whilst brushing
His shirt to get the dirt off
He showed no sign
Of hurt
His eyes still
Searching the Terra-firma

"They killed Anika"
Eugene pants
As if chanting in disbelief
The rain drops
That hit his cheeks
Hid the grief

"You what?"
Omar growls
"No!"
He rips viciously
Teeth snapping
Like an angry dog
An anger that hid his misery

He pauses

His eye lids flutter
His lips stripped of speech
He walks towards a tree
He sits
His head dips
He weeps

"Am sorry"
Eugene says
"It's not your fault"
Omar pouts
"I just hope that speech
You made
Inspires someone to help us out"

"Where's Kamari?"
Eugene stutters
On noticing
His absence
"Captured"
Omar responds
"His car crashed
The wardens
Grabbed him

He saved my life"
He continues
The sadness
Flowing down his face
"They'll probably
Probe him for information
And then throw him
Into an estate"

Second's pass in silence
Then Eugene spots
A shimmer of light
Glistening in the grass
Omar's medallion
Catches his sight

He picks up the broken chain
The locket opens
There's a picture in the frame
A picture that he recognises
As…

"Daisy?"

He exclaims

"Hey!?"
Omar says
"How do you know that name?"

"My brother…"
Eugene responds
"Erm…
I met her at the Cedar Estate"

"The One has truly brought us together"
Omar whispers
With passion in his speaking

"There are no coincidences
Everything happens for a reason"

He jumps up
And rushes
Through the bushes
Towards
The place he had parked
Eugene chases
After him
Until they
Make it to the car

Where a
Matte black hummer
Is sitting
Right behind Omar's truck
On the license plate
Hunter
Is written
The window broke
After Omar struck

His arm through
He opens it up
He gets in
Slams
Hard with the door
A key drops from the visor
He inserts it
The engine starts with a roar

"Get in kid"
Omar calls
Eugene jumps in beside fast
"Where are we going?"
Eugene asks
"I've got a plan
To get my wife back"

Skidding wheels screech
Causing water from the tar to spray
They speed back
Towards the settlement
And park
Next to the gold arbor archway

They jog down the winding path
Fast
As the sound of
Thunder moans
They run
Through the wood
Until they make it to the bungalow

Omar opens the door and
Shoves Eugene inside
"Stay here" he says
Then he locks the door behind

"Am going to get Daisy"
He shouts
"How?"
Eugene calls
Confused
"Am going to pay a visit
 To Mortimer"
Omar replies
"I've got an offer
He can't refuse"

18. BACK AT THE BEGINNING

"It was you
Omar"
Eugene mumbles
Waking slowly
"It was you who let them know"
"I got you what you want Mortimer"
Omar says
"Now let her go"

The moon glows

Eugene's eyes blink hazily
Opening then closing
As he slowly woke
From his comatose

His head feeling
As though
It was exploding
From the blow

Lightning strikes
And thunder groans
He remembers running
From those two hunters
And though his run was stunted
He had made it quite far from the bungalow

He lay close to the woods
Blunt
There's a baby crying
Somewhere outside of his eyesight
And a distant belt for help
Sounds like Grant's
Still stuck in the sky light

Omar and Mortimer
Stand over Eugene
Out of focus
In a blur
Eugene had been remembering
All events that had occurred

Events that had passed
Which brought them to this position
The collision with Omar's axe
Had reversed his cognition

Lightning strikes
Eugene sits up
From being
Sprawled on the grass
There's the sound of
Rapid rain tapping
Mortimer's hat

Daisy's there
Wriggling
Stuck
In a warden's clasp
She's holding crying baby
Trying to escape
But trying in vain

The rasp of the thunderclap
Rumbles
Frank the hunter arrives
"E's not arf fast"
He laughs
His hungered lungs pulling
In chunks of air as he gasps

"You turned out to be quite the pest
Eugene" Mortimer says
Squatting down with glum scowl
"Look around" he whispers
"There's nowhere to run now"

"Let my wife go"
Omar yells
"I got you the boy
We had a deal"
"A deal?"
Mortimer squeals mockingly
Then his face converts to cold steel

"No deal" he growls
"Did you really think
 It'd be that easy
Did you really think I'd make a deal
And miss out on a catch
This peachy?" He grins

"A whole community of undesirables
Wait till Dean Jiles learns of this
The honor I'll be awarded
The fame
The riches"

"Omar?
What have you done?"
Eugene asks deflated
"Please forgive me"
Omar states
"I used you as the bait kid
But I needed to save Daisy"

"And what a mistake
You've made"
Mortimer laughs
His eyes blazing
As bright as suns
"Now we'll have a ball
You've given me
All for the price
Of one"

"Arrest them"
He orders
And Frank pounces to joust with Omar
Omar throws his axe down
And bounds forth to bulldoze the ogre

They smash together with a massive rasping tremor
Another lightning strike
Heightens their clash
The weather
Frightening

The wind changes
From a cowering zephyr
To a growling aggressor

Wrestling
Omar and the hunter
Grapple close
Frank throws a flurry of punches
But Omar dodges the blows

Then throws one of his own
Which lands
Spot on the nose of Frank
He wobbles
Then
Launches a thump full throttle
That sinks into Omar's flank

Omar kneels
Omar stands

Omar uses swatting hands
To block Franks
Gangly kicking legs
But one lands and hits his head
It flings him hard
Down to the earth
With pounding sound
Resounding loud

He murmurs
Word as if in hurt
Falling
Through the grass
And to the ground

Eugene bounces to his feet
But
Mortimer's quick to cease his zest
He unsheathes a sword
From his walking stick
And points the tip
At Eugene's chest

"Another step and you're dead meat"
He slyly says
With smiling face
As Frank
Picks a slightly dazed Omar
Out of the grass
By his braids

"We made you undesirable
By blaming you
For our crimes"
Mortimer growls
"Why?"
Eugene asks
"To create fear"
Mortimer replies

"You lovers are too attracting
Too much hope
Too much soul
If that gets into city folk
They'll be impossible to control

But thanks to Omar's love
For this here pretty girl
We can put an end to you lovers
And continue to dominate the world"

"Never"
Eugene rips

"Yes"
Mortimer's reply blurts
"He's given me you
And the settlement
In exchange for his wife unhurt

What a dirty
Trick he's played"
Mortimer says
Looking Omar in the eyes
"The irony is
He's going to be
The first to die

Finish him"

Mortimer smiles
Commanding Frank
To commence foul
And with a growl
Frank turns Omar around
With intent to disembowel

"Omar!"
Daisy calls
Her fight more intense now
She ploughs
Her head
Into the warden's mouth

POW!!!

She breaks free
With wailing
Alarmed
Flailing armed baby
Encased in her arms
She races towards
Omar
In an attempt
To save him from harm

The warden chases
Cupping his bloodied lip
Eugene kicks out a foot
And trips the warden
Into Mortimer
Knocking the sword walking stick
Out of his grip

Frank stalls

"Daisy's free"
Omar calls
"Daisy's free"
Again he bawls
And with this call
The bushes start to rustle
And lovers
Emerge in a swarm

Lovers
The lovers from the settlement
Strewed
They had used the woods
As cover
Just waiting for their cue
To move

Mortimer
Reaches to the ground
To collect the sword
For his protect
But Eugene
Beats him to it
And directs the tip
At Mortimer's neck

Mortimer
Raises his hands
In surrender
And
Surprise

Eugene has
An intense sense of resent
In his vibe
And revenge
In his eyes

"You killed Lewis!"
He rages
"Yes"
Mortimer's empty reply
Despite the threat to his life
He made
No attempt to disguise
His contemptuous side

"Then you must die"
Eugene says
The blade touching Mortimer's throat
Mortimer doesn't flinch
And then…

"EUGENE DON'T!!!"

A shout that
Travels
Across the grassy plain
And came to Eugene
Booming
Loud
It's the voice of Laith
Who is pushing his way
Through the crowd

Moving scouts
Out of his path
Others making way freely
His cane helping his
Careful steps
He creeps towards Eugene
Neatly

He gently touches his arm
"Eugene"
No response deployed
"Put it down" he says
"This is exactly what he wants my boy"

"Their plan for us
Is to anger us
And bring about revenge reactions
Proving that we are criminals
Which would further justify our extraction"

"Am going to finish him
Once and for all"
Eugene says with fiery eyes
In steamed glasses
"It's time to take
Our lives back"
He says
"I'm tired of being passive"

"We are not passive"
Laith says
"We trust that
Justice will be served
But to take action
Into your own hands
Would only make things worse

A lover must be patient
In all situations
Every action must be taken
In wisdom and with grace
Actions made in haste
Can be made to be complacent
Causing complication
Or resulting in distaste"
He says

"Put the saber down
My boy
Let the One destroy the sordid
And know
No oppression
Goes unpunished and no good
Goes unrewarded

We only seek love
To love and protect
These tyrants
Will get their comeuppance
If not this life
Then the next"

Omar flexes
Vexed
His eyes glow to a smolder
And with a quick swipe
And a roll
He throws Frank over his shoulder
Then hits him with a knockout
"Laith's right"
He shouts
"Don't do it
Put it down kid
There's no way he can
Cause any harm now
We have them surrounded"

"This was my plan precisely"
He grins
"It's come together nicely
It wasn't just a plan to free my wife
But the whole estate"
He cites

"After I locked you
In the bungalow
I went straight to Laiths hut
To wake him up
And explained
That Daisy was at the Cedar Estate
And I had a scheme
To save them but
I needed help

I hoped they would exchange
You for Daisy
Well…
That's the feeling I felt
And I knew if
I told Mortimer
About the settlement
He'd want to see it himself

I knew the thought
And concept of conquest
Would enrapture him
The aim was to lure him here
So we could capture him"

"You swine"
Mortimer sneers

"Now we have their
Leader restrained"
Omar eagerly says
"The wardens at the Cedar Estate
Will be like a body in need of a brain

We could march there leisurely"
He smiles
"Overthrow gleefully
And free all the people in the estate
Quite easily
To try and do it on your own
Would have been a grueling endeavor
Look around"
He says

"Eugene
We can do this…Together"

Swayed
Eugene steps back
In a show of reframe
Rain drops sliding off
The metal as he lowers the blade

"You will regret this Eugene"
Mortimer says
As he's surrounded
By lovers
Who put his hands in chains
And his feet in restraints

"Take them away"
Laith commands
"And keep them under arrest
But though
They may detest us
Make sure you treat them as guests"

Just as he says
A group of big
Brave looking
Lovers takes them away
At quick pace
They carry Franks
Limp frame
Free Grant from the window
And march
Them all
Towards the lift
At the cliffs face

"How can you treat
Them with any sort of respect"
Eugene protests
"After all of the harm they've caused
All the distress
All of his threats"

"Sure" Laith says
"We could practice revenge tactics
But then
We would be just as bad as them
In their fanatics
Their way is to hate
So
They centre the harsh
Our way is to show respect
In hope
Love enters the hearts"

"Hey
Maybe we could use them
In the future
As bait
To catch other fish"
Omar says
But for now
"I think it's time to go and free your
Mother kid"

19. TOMORROW

The copper coloured
Sun rises
Over the horizon
Filling the sky with golden life

Rain drops that hold
Rays of light
Roll
Over leaves
Cling
To empty branches
Then fall near to where
Flowers are unfolding
Stretching to welcome the day

Fifty firm faced
Lovers make their way toward
The Cedar Estate
Marching through
The brightening woodlands
Omar leading the way

Eugene striding beside him
Darkness hiding on light arriving
Songs of love

And
Chants of
"All are in need of One
One is in need of none"
Slammed
From this grand band

They sight the clearing
To the estate
And on nearing
They hear
Cheering
Blearing

Omar puts his hand
In the air
"Wait"
He calls
And on his command
All the marching
Comes to a stand

Eugene breaks ranks
And goes veering
Ahead
Using the bushes as cover
As he peers through a piercing

And there
Outside the Cedar Estate gate
A mob of people
In a state of celebrate

An array of yays
And hurray
Ablaze

City folk and lovers
Together
Engaging
Embracing

The gates
Are open
There are lovers flowing out
A glow of hope on faces
Once filled with brokenness
And doubt

Eugene looks
For the wardens
But
There are none of them about
He looks around for his mum and brother
Neither are found within his scout

He bursts into the crowd
Weaving through
Eager
Seeking like a seeker
Then to his relief he sees her

She's leaning against a tree
Holding the baby closely
Jerome's hovering over the bushes
Excitedly picking peonies

Eugene rushes over
Glee moving his spirit
"Mum"
He yells
"You did it Eugene
You did it"
She says
As they embrace

Jerome joins
They hold with care
So close and
So near
No space for the cold air

"These city folk"
She says in disbelief
They must have took to your words"
"All thanks to the One"
Eugene replies
"As Omar and the
Others emerge"

"Lewis"
She sobs
"He's gone"
She confirms
Both Eugene's
Eyes well up
"I know" he returns

"What happened here?"
He asks
She unhands him
And steps to the tree
"These city folk
Came marching here"
She says
"Demanding they set us free

That one is their leader"
She adds
Pointing into the crowd
At a short mousy looking lady
Brown freckled face
Standing proud

Afro puffs
Round glasses
Her eyes host the look of thunder
The words 'Mellow Rebel'
Printed on her
Yellow hooded jumper

"The wardens were outnumbered"
Mary says
"The city folk
Belted for change
And one of the soft-hearted wardens
Well
He must have felt the same

Because he just opened the gate
And let us all go ahead
Not even a fist was lifted
The wardens they just fled

These city folk say it's the beginning
They're saying it full of chest
They want to join forces
They want to free the rest

They came here just like soldiers
That girl led with such composure"
Mary pauses her flow of speech
"Eugene
It looks as though
She's coming over"

And she was

She was marching
At pace
Staring Eugene
In the face
Her smile says
Kind hearted
Her stride says
No time to waste

"Eugene!"
She calls
"I don't know where the point
Of bravery ends
And the point of crazy starts
But what I do know
Is your little stunt has won our hearts"

She puts her hand out
For Eugene to shake it
He takes it
A smile of relief
Lights his face

"I'm Ruby"
She introduces
And this is the resistance"
She points towards
The group assisting
Lovers in the distance

"Thank you"
Eugene beams
"No
Thank *you*"
Ruby replies
"Your selflessness
Inspired us
You've saved so many lives

For years
We've resisted
We never believe
What these tyrants say
We saw you on our screens
And knew we had to come right away

We came ready to fight today
We had fighting in our sights today
But your words
Proved more powerful than any striking blade

If we can get these people to safety
We could try and save others
We could spread the love
Among city folk
And join forces with our brothers

"Great minds think alike"
Omar says
As he
Strides beside
With pride
"I was thinking that
Together
We could try
Free one estate at a time"

"What about Dean Jiles?"
Eugene says
Whilst looking upwards
Facing the sky
"One day"
Omar replies
"He'll be made to pay
For his crimes"

Eugene's eyes tracing
Following a leaf
That's falling with
A gracious sway
"And what about us?"
Mary asks
"We've got no place to stay"

"There's plenty space
At the settlement"
Omar smiles
"You'll be safe with us there" he says
"Let's round everyone up
And head there straight away"

He counts at the crowd

"A few adjustments
Could make it happen…
…Obviously
We might have to
Build a few extra cabins"
He laughs

Jerome tugs Omar's shirt
"Excuse me sir
I have a request
I was just wondering"
He stutters
"Does the settlement need a chef?"
Omar's head hangs over
To take view of the young man
Who's standing with a smile
And plush purple peonies
In his hand

"Yep
We're definitely
Going to need
Your skills my clever lad"
"Good"
Jerome says
"Because I make the very best stew
You've ever had"

Eugene
Tracks the garnet coloured leaf
Twisting with the breeze
Dipping and then lifting
Like a ship drifting
Through the seas

He sticks his arm out quickly
As a gust makes it arc sharply
It's twists and turns
With zest
And then
It rests in his palm calmly

"We have to spread love"
He says
"We have to work together
And through today's struggle
I know

TOMORROW WILL BE BETTER"

Eugene

Abdul Malik:

Being a fan of hip-hop music as a youth, **he began writing** rhymes **at the age of 12**. After becoming a Muslim in 2011, **he fell in love with the ways,** works **and poetry of Sufi poets** such as Rumi, Shams Tabrizi and ibn Arabi. He has since been putting his experiences and expressions into poetry. His writing is focused around seeking peace and divine love but he also speaks on social and societal issues.

He says: *"I only hope that sharing these insights, poems and stories will help others to find their place of peace. Maybe we will meet each other there."*

Other work by the author:

Returning The Flower

A compilation of poems and meditations to connect and inspire.

The Message of Muhammad ﷺ

Beautiful statements of the Prophet Muhammad ﷺ with calming patterns to colour

Join the mailing list today for updates by visiting

www.abdulmalikwriting.co.uk

9 781999 843229